YOUNG & SOBER

Stories by Those Who Found AA Early

From the Pages of AA Grapevine

BOOKS PUBLISHED BY
AA GRAPEVINE, INC.

The Language of the Heart (& eBook)
The Best of Bill (& eBook)
Spiritual Awakenings (& eBook)
I Am Responsible: The Hand of AA
The Home Group: Heartbeat of AA
Emotional Sobriety: The Next Frontier (& eBook)
Spiritual Awakenings II (& eBook)
In Our Own Words: Stories of Young AAs in Recovery
Beginners' Book
Voices of Long-Term Sobriety
A Rabbit Walks into a Bar
Step by Step: Real AAs, Real Recovery (& eBook)
Emotional Sobriety II: The Next Frontier (& eBook)
Young & Sober (& eBook)

IN SPANISH

El Lenguaje del Corazón
Lo Mejor de Bill (& eBook)
Lo Mejor de La Viña
El Grupo Base: Corazón de AA

IN FRENCH

Les meilleurs articles de Bill
Le Langage du coeur
Le Groupe d'attache: Le battement du coeur des AA

YOUNG & SOBER

Stories by Those Who Found AA Early

From the Pages of AA Grapevine

AAGRAPEVINE,Inc.
New York, New York
WWW.AAGRAPEVINE.ORG

AA PREAMBLE

Alcoholics Anonymous is a fellowship of men and women
who share their experience, strength and hope
with each other that they may solve their common problem
and help others to recover from alcoholism.

The only requirement for membership is a desire to stop drinking.
There are no dues or fees for AA membership;
we are self-supporting through our own contributions.
AA is not allied with any sect, denomination, politics, organization
or institution; does not wish to engage in any controversy,
neither endorses nor opposes any causes.

Our primary purpose is to stay sober
and help other alcoholics to achieve sobriety.

©AA Grapevine, Inc.

CONTENTS

CHAPTER ONE
WHAT IT WAS LIKE, WHAT HAPPENED
Their drinking careers weren't long—but long enough

CHAPTER TWO
I EARNED MY SEAT
Young, but no less an alcoholic

CHAPTER THREE
THE NEXT GENERATION
Growing up around AA is no guarantee against alcoholism

CHAPTER EIGHT
LIVING LIFE, GROWING UP
Through good times and bad, these AAs turn to the Fellowship
and their Higher Powers and keep going

CHAPTER NINE
A FEW 24 HOURS LATER
Young old-timers talk about where their journey has taken them,
and about passing it on to the next generation

WELCOME

Young & Sober is a collection of Grapevine stories about the joys and challenges of recovering early in life, and about recognizing alcoholism after a drinking history that in some cases has only lasted a few years. Are the stories of those who came to AA in their teens, 20s and 30s different from those who got sober later in life? No ... and yes. "Being young, we recover fast physically," writes the author of, "Young Peoples' Groups." "But our insides still boil like mad ... the young person ... has little or no productive past, and organizing a life terrorizes him."

Chapters One and Two are a collection of qualifications—the places drinking took young alcoholics and examples of how they earned their seat at the table. Chapters Three through Five explore relationships with family members who have long been part of AA, with old-timers who helped show them the ropes, and finally, with people their own age.

Chapters Six and Seven talk about further coming to grips with alcoholism and recovery from it. Several writers did not fully accept their disease until some event finally got their attention. Some describe how getting involved in service helped them feel more a part of things, while others write about how working the Steps showed them a way out of their misery. "What we are like now" is covered in Chapters Eight and Nine, with topics such as acceptance, growing up, growing older, and experiencing joy and pain in sobriety. "Having the opportunity to watch this program work in young peoples' lives the way that it worked in mine is one of the greatest joys of my sobriety," says the author of "Fountain of Youth." Written by alcoholics of all lengths of sobriety, Young & Sober is about coming into AA at an early age, learning to have sober relationships, doing the Steps and getting service commitments—and most of all, it's about learning how to live life joyously.

CHAPTER ONE

WHAT IT WAS LIKE, WHAT HAPPENED

Their drinking careers weren't long—but long enough

What brings an alcoholic through the doors of an AA meeting? What brings a young person, perhaps still working his or her way through high school, into the basement of a church, into a meeting room where the other members there are often older, married with children, established in a career, engaged in community activities?

"No way was I going to spend all my time with those old fogies. They were all over twenty-five!" one member recounts in "Nothing Left to Lose." But after more experimentation, more problems, and several more treatment centers, she returns.

"My options were very obvious: jail, the streets, or death. I was also suffering from liver disease," the author of the story, "Homeless Bound" says. For him the repercussions of drinking were concrete and physical. For others, the devastation was more emotional and internal. "I couldn't bear to look in the mirror," writes the author of "Teen Nightmare."

These and the other AAs in this Chapter, as well as throughout this book, have drinking histories that anyone can identify with. "I never went anywhere without a mug full of whiskey and cola. All but one of my friends had had enough of my erratic, violent, and rude behavior while drinking. I always drank to get as drunk as I could."

The age they came into AA or the length of time they spent drinking are, in fact, small details. It is the loneliness, the alienation, the humiliation and sickness that comes from drinking alcoholically that finally brings them in, or finally convinces them to stay. "Alcoholism has no minimum age requirement. I realize that many fellow AA members have lost homes, marriages, and children to alcohol before I acquired any of those things. But I lost enough."

Young or old, newcomers or old-timers, there is something of all of our stories here.

NOTICED
OCTOBER 2007

I had my first drink when I was twelve years old. I loved it. I loved the way it made me feel, and the way it made me not feel. I grew up yearning for a place to belong, and when I drank, I found it. My first drink allowed me to become someone completely different. It allowed me to have a voice, and believe me, people heard it. It made me feel like I finally was being noticed, and I never looked back.

At first, I drank just on weekends. I looked forward to Friday every week. I dropped out of school in eighth grade, and took up drinking instead. I never drank socially. I always drank to get as drunk as I could, as fast as I could. I didn't care what I was drinking, as long as I was going to get drunk.

When I was thirteen, I made a pitiful attempt at suicide. I took a large bottle of extra-strength acetaminophen. I don't think I really wanted to die, because I phoned my best friend an hour later and told her what I'd done. I was desperate to be seen, to be noticed. I especially wanted my mother to see me. But all she did was tell me to go and drink some coffee and then go to bed. I ended up in the hospital for a couple of days, with a social worker telling me I was crying out for help. I went home feeling embarrassed and stupid. I didn't care about anything. I drank right away, too.

By this time, alcohol had taken hold of me. I went back to school for a year and then left—I had a hard time with teachers and authority. That was just an excuse at the time, though. I really just wanted to drink and be cool. At fifteen, I got pregnant. I didn't drink for the nine months that I was pregnant, but it was all I thought about. I wanted to have the baby so that I could get on with drinking again. When I did have the baby, I got drunk a month later. I tried to breast-feed, but couldn't do that and drink, so I eliminated the breast-feed-ing. That's how it was for the next few years.

I went back to school twice, but quit both times. Alcohol consumed my whole life. I went from weekend drinking with my friends to drinking almost every day, alone. I wasn't the best parent all the time, either. It was as if I had absolutely no morals when I drank. I didn't care about anyone or anything except getting the next drink. This included my son. Most of the time, I left him at home with my mom while I went out and partied. When he woke up in the middle of the night, my mom would call me to come home. I would go home, but just to get my son and bring him back to the party. That was the insanity of my drinking.

I had no God in my life, except when life was going badly. Then I begged God for help. When it didn't come, I hated him. I certainly didn't have any real faith. Then, in July 2000, I ended up in a hospital in four-point restraints, ready to be committed to the psych ward. I was more drunk than I'd ever been before, and I had left my son at someone's house, and then forgotten about him. As a result, I was under investigation by the Ministry of Social Services. I thought my life was over. I begged God to get me out of this one, and I would never do it again. I wished that it had all been a bad nightmare and that I would wake up. But the reality was that I was in big trouble and alcohol had gotten me there.

My therapist came and released me from the hospital and took me home. I had to call an alcohol and drug counselor in order to get out of trouble with the Ministry of Social Services. I swore to myself and everybody else that I was never going to drink again. Never.

I was drunk that night. I couldn't figure out how it happened, or why. When I called the counselor the next day, she told me that I was a binge drinker and that I should get some help. I was very angry, but a seed was planted.

I wasn't quite ready to quit drinking, but every time I drank, I wondered whether I was an alcoholic or not. I drank for another month after that, and it got worse. All I could think about was getting drunk and how to get the money to get drunk. I even spent my son's savings.

My last drunk wasn't my worst drunk. It wasn't even anything special. But that morning, I had a moment of clarity—my spiritual awakening. I looked in a mirror and saw that there was nothing left inside of me. My family wanted nothing to do with me, and neither did the family of my son's father. I was ashamed, and full of guilt and fear. As I was walking down a flight of stairs, I heard a voice inside my head. It said, "My name is Rosie, and I am an alcoholic." I don't think it was my voice. I think it was my Higher Power's voice. But when I heard it, I thought of Alcoholics Anonymous. I looked up central office's number and called. Somebody picked me up that night and took me to my first meeting. That was August 24, 2000.

My favorite thing about Alcoholics Anonymous is the genuineness. People are honest and they care. I have earned trust. I have learned to trust and to love. I am the secretary of my home group. Every so often, I speak about alcoholism and AA in high schools. I finally finished twelfth grade.

All my life I searched for a purpose, and now I've found it. I need to carry the message of Alcoholics Anonymous to others so they will have the same chance at life that I did. My son now has a chance at life, too, and I am forever indebted to AA for that.

ROSIE B.
NANAIMO, BRITISH COLUMBIA

TEEN NIGHTMARE
OCTOBER 2011

I was already emotionally unstable before I started my career as an alcoholic. Both of my parents were born in Mexico. My parents split when I was about 13. I was happy as a child, but I just went wild. My dad had left the state with his new girlfriend. Now it was just my mom, my sister, and me. I was a freshman when I started drinking, and that same year I started cutting myself.

The following years were nothing but parties, cruising in stranger's cars, fights with the family and a lot of self-destructive behavior. At 16, I became bulimic. I made myself throw up because I felt ugly. Within a year, I was hospitalized at a mental hospital for the third time because of suicide attempts. I have been in and out of AA since I was 16. I worked with a drug counselor, a therapist, and a psychiatrist and they diagnosed me as a bipolar manic-depressive. I was prescribed a variety of meds to help keep me stabilized. The only pills I felt OK with were the mood stabilizers because they helped with my intense emotions and anxiety.

After a relapse when I was 17, I drank with all of my medications. I was heavily drunk when I decided to gulp them. This happened a night before my mom's birthday. I thought my life was over. I was just so tired of waking up and seeing my world dark and clouded. I couldn't bear to look in the mirror. I was numb. I felt as if my life was an endless movie of self-destruction, rejection and abuse—something unreal. It became so unbearable that I finally just gave up. I stayed sober for 13 months and relapsed a few weeks before my 19th birthday. I stayed out for two months and realized that even if I didn't feel like killing myself, even if I had all the things I wanted and was fit and healthy, alcohol and drugs were not going to clean up the mess I created. I was throwing my life away. Maybe, just maybe, I don't know so much about living life.

Today I am in service every single day—from the moment I wake up to the hour I go to bed. Today I try to be honest with myself so that I know what my real intentions are.

At first being thoroughly honest was hard. I didn't like admitting to humans, God and myself the exact nature of my defects. I still don't like admitting that I'm powerless over everything and everyone. I still don't accept that my life is unmanageable on a daily basis. But all of this is becoming easier for me to do by practicing it and following suggestions from my sponsor. Whenever things get hard, or I don't want to follow through with a suggestion, I simply humble myself to my Higher Power and say, "Just for today." That helps me live in the moment, and accept that—just for today—AA is my reality. I didn't need meds to stay sober, just a Higher Power, a spiritual path and someone to hold my hand through it all. AA has given that to me.

EDUARDO C.
SAN JOSÉ, CALIFORNIA

WIPED OUT
JUNE 1997

My drinking career may seem short to some. It lasted about twelve years, starting when I was fourteen. I could buy anything, anywhere because I was six feet four inches tall and weighed 200 pounds. I was every father's nightmare of his daughter's date.

I can't tell you what I was like at the end. I have no memory of it. A year of my life has been completely wiped out. I can only tell you what it did to me. When I came out of intensive care, I weighed only 130 pounds. I was in a wheelchair. It wasn't a car accident that put me there; I had crawled into a bottle and almost killed myself. From what I've been able to find out, the doctors think I drank for about two months, day and night.

The alcohol level in my body was toxic enough to cause me to quit breathing four or five times. My internal organs (liver, etc.) had shut down. My body wasn't functioning. That and the alcohol poisoning are what put me in the wheelchair. My vocal cords were paralyzed, my voice only a whisper. My memory was shot to hell.

After a year in the wheelchair, I was able to start using forearm crutches. I used them for four months before I could walk on my own. My voice is back and I'm able to shout with the best of them. The memory is still bad but I deal with it. I have used the stubbornness that kept me drinking to aid in my recovery. I have a lot of tangible things that I can look at and say, "Things are better."

I'm not going to say that it is all better. Even with everything I've been through, it will cross my mind to drink again. I'm not sure that this desire will ever leave me. I call it a gut reaction. The old-timers that I've met at the meetings are split over whether it will ever go away. Right now I work on realizing that what I can control is my reaction to that thought. I also look at meetings as getting together with friends; that way it isn't a chore. It is something that I want to do. I don't know if I can risk a relapse; I came very close to death with my last drink. Now there are people around me who will help me, and maybe I've helped them.

Bad things will still happen; that is life. But I get to live it. That's something I took for granted at one time and almost lost. In November I had my two-year anniversary. It doesn't sound like much but at the beginning I didn't think it was possible. I did it a day at a time as it was suggested. It has worked so far so I don't plan on changing it.

RICK A.
EL PASO, TEXAS

PREAMBLE TO RECOVERY
MAY 1975

We put the AA Preamble in the *Labor News*, a once-a-week paper. Last week, a man who left AA twenty years ago happened to read it. Even though he was drunk, he got hold of another AA member and went to his first meeting again. And last night at a meeting, a friend told me he was still sober. I guess that makes it all worthwhile.

When I came around the first time at age sixteen, I just couldn't identify with anyone. AA wasn't out in the open as much. Then I came back at twenty-five, in January 1970, after living two years on Clark Street in Chicago. There still weren't any real young people in AA. The youngest were in their thirties. But I made up my mind to stay anyway. I've only had one slip since then, at the end of two years, simply because I didn't work the Steps. I was lucky it only lasted six days.

After my slip, I started working all Twelve Steps in order, and I lost my compulsion to drink, even when I went through a lot emotionally. My wife came down with Guillain-Barré syndrome. It's a form of polio. She was completely paralyzed for eight months and out of work for a year. I had only been sober about four months when she became ill, and you know, I didn't even think of a drink, even when she was in intensive care and they didn't know whether she would live or not. If it hadn't been for AA, I wouldn't have made it.

Last September, my wife had our first child—a boy. So, you see, I'm really thankful for AA, because it gave me my wife and son. I met my wife, who is a nurse, while on a Twelfth Step call. We had taken a fellow to the hospital for help.

When I was young, I was a wino on the street for two years, in mental hospitals about forty times, and in jails about as often. It got so bad, the AAs didn't want me, 'cause I had used them so many times. I was even barred from the hospital at the end. I'm grateful that this past Christmas I didn't have to sleep outside in a back alley where it was twenty below zero. In fact, I'm grateful to be around at all. On one of my drunks, while on skid row, I passed out on top of a railroad trestle and was run over by a freight train. When I came to, the only thing I thought of was whether my wine bottle was busted.

In January, I had my third anniversary. Now, we see a lot of younger people and other people who didn't have to go down as far as I did, and I'm glad. I just wish that everyone knew about AA, but a lot of people still don't. Putting the Preamble in the paper might help someone else someplace else. We put the AA central office phone number at the bottom, and they got some calls.

W. C.
ROCKFORD, ILLINOIS

HOMELESS BOUND
NOVEMBER 2008

It was August 1977. I was homeless and facing life in prison. With thirty-five cents in my pocket and nowhere to live, my options were very obvious: jail, the streets, or death. I was also suffering from liver disease.

I had just spent the night at my sister's home in Queens, New York. My mom had snuck me in; I had been thrown out of a close friend's house the night before; I'd fallen asleep with a cigarette and nearly burned his house down. He threw me out and asked that I not return.

In my semi-blackout, I made it to my sister's house. I woke up at about six in the morning. I looked up at a figure in front of me and realized it was my sister. Before I could even think, she told me I would have to leave. "I don't trust you, Richard," she said. I was not welcome there anymore.

This was devastating. Where was I going to go? I had burned every bridge I had. I'd hurt all the people and friends who'd tried to help me.

In just a few minutes, I was walking out the door to my obscurity. I had no destination at all. I had a bag full of soiled clothes as dirty as the ones I was wearing. I weighed 135 pounds soaking wet.

Then my bottom came. I didn't hear the storm door close behind me. I knew my mom was watching, and my heart was breaking more and more with each step I took from her. I didn't want to look into her eyes. I didn't have any more room for pain. I was dead inside, scared of everything. I turned and saw her looking, and we both cried. We knew this was not going to be easy for me.

I walked about a mile, to a luncheonette where the owner knew my sister. He saw that I was strung out, and he made me a milkshake. He also gave me a pack of cigarettes. I sat pondering what I was going to do with my life. I had no strength to go back to the old neighborhood, I was too ashamed to ask anyone for money to get a drink, and I didn't want to, anyway.

It was humid, hot, and just downright ugly. I wanted to lie down and cry. I was alone and scared to death. How could this happen to a twenty-three-year-old boy? That's right, I was still a boy. Alcoholism had been killing me since my birth. My older brother had gone to this place called AA. Maybe they can help me, I thought.

In a few minutes, I'd dropped a dime into a pay phone; I wound up in a meeting that afternoon. The miracles—too many to mention—began with that call. I was a rarity when I came into the rooms. I had a heroin addiction, and I was the youngest man in the group. Back then, they didn't accept that easily, but no one judged me. I respected the Traditions, and they healed me back to life.

Within five years, I was free of all criminal charges. I have been sober twenty-five years. I have achieved more than I ever thought possible in my life.

RICHARD D.
LONG BEACH, NEW YORK

NOTHING LEFT TO LOSE
MARCH 1997

"I spilled more than you ever drank," said a man with three years of sobriety and three million grey hairs. My alcoholic mind used that phrase to excuse my next drunk. I was fourteen years old and thought I was too young to be an alcoholic. I'm sixteen years old now and know alcoholism has no minimum age requirement. I realize that many fellow AA members have lost homes, marriages, and children to alcohol before I acquired any of those things. But I lost enough.

I drank for the first time when I was ten years old. I looked and acted sixteen at the time. I was a lot taller and more mature than the other kids. When I was drunk I could be any age I wanted. By the time I was eleven I'd do anything for any guy who would buy me a bottle. I was hanging out with twenty-year-old hookers by the time I was twelve. That was when I was put into a treatment center. I spent thirty days there learning the right answers and looking forward intently to my next drunk.

During the next year I never went anywhere without a mug full of whiskey and cola. Somehow I wasn't picked up for prostitution or driving under the influence without a driver's license. I was usually the designated driver because I was the only one who wasn't passed out by the time everyone had to go home.

Again, I was put into a treatment center where I spent sixty days. There I was introduced to Alcoholics Anonymous. No way was I going to spend all my time with those old fogies. They were all over twenty-five! After my sixty days of patience, I once again went out and got plowed.

During the next six months I remember three days. Those three days were filled with suicidal thoughts that I was too scared to fulfill because I thought I'd go to hell for all the people I'd hurt. Once again I was placed in a treatment center. Once again I got drunk. I realized I might have a problem when I drank all of my friend's beer and was throwing up on his shoes.

Thanks to my many trips through treatment I decided once again to try Alcoholics Anonymous. I didn't have anything to lose. I did what people told me to do: went to ninety meetings in ninety days, got a sponsor, started to work the Steps, and read the Big Book. My sponsor said this was "willingness," but I preferred to call it "going to any lengths." I now have almost a year in Alcoholics Anonymous. I love to spend time with the people in the Fellowship whom I used to think were "old fogies." Every day I thank my Higher Power for them and their acceptance of me.

And occasionally, when I meet someone who says they spilled more than I ever drank, I politely reply, "Perhaps if you hadn't spilled so much, you would have gotten here sooner."

SUNNY B.
BOUNTIFUL, UTAH

THE ONLY FAILURE
DEAR GRAPEVINE, MARCH 1981

I'm a twenty-six-year-old alcoholic and drug addict—and very grateful I came back to the program of Alcoholics Anonymous.

I found out early that I couldn't drink like other people. Since booze caused so much trouble, I decided to experiment with drugs. For the next ten years, I mixed booze with drugs and landed in some pretty sordid spots—jails, hospitals, the street.

Four years ago, I was introduced to AA. I was going to learn from your mistakes and learn how to drink decent, like most other people. At twenty-two, I could readily admit I had a problem with alcohol and that my life had become unmanageable. But to take never having another drink of booze? Never! It's taken me four years to learn that I don't take that first drink today.

I'm grateful that I still have my family, health, and youth. And after this last slip, I'm grateful for AAs who told me that the only failure in the program is the failure to come back.

V. L.
TEXAS

SOMEDAY I'LL BE CURED
JANUARY 2003

When I look at what my life is like today compared to the way it was going seven years ago, I'm amazed. Seven years ago, I couldn't stop drinking although I desperately wanted to. All but one of my friends had had enough of my erratic, violent, and rude behavior while drinking. I ate barely enough to keep me going; eating made getting drunk a slower process, and I needed to get drunk as fast as possible. I also wanted to die, but I couldn't think of a foolproof way to do it. I couldn't bear the thought of the shame I would feel if I tried to commit suicide again and failed. I didn't really want to die, but I didn't know that till I'd been sober quite some time. What I wanted was to have my life changed, but I didn't believe that anything but death could change it.

Thankfully, I did find an alternative to suicide. In 1995, I found AA and have been sober ever since. Oh, I knew about AA long before 1995. My father had gotten sober several years previously; in fact, the year he got sober was the year I started drinking in earnest. He took me to open meetings and although I knew in my head that alcoholism wasn't about willpower, I didn't believe it in my heart. I believed I could drink differently, so I got drunk for the first time at age twelve. I never want to forget that night. I remember thinking, I've found it. This is what I need to feel okay. For the first time that I could remember I felt that I was okay, that everyone else was okay, and that the world was a safe and fair place. That was before I blacked out and was sexually assaulted.

I made a decision before the blackout to drink as much and as often as possible. The next morning, when I heard what had happened while I was blacked out, I felt deeply ashamed. I thought that guy's taking advantage of my drunken vulnerability was my fault. And there began the pattern that defined my drinking. I always drank to get drunk. I always blacked out and did, or had something done to me, that made me feel ashamed. And then I needed to drink more to bury the shame that got bigger every time I drank.

My drinking continued that way for the next seven years. I got sober at age nineteen, only nine months after I became legally able to drink. Before reaching that age, I drank as much as I could, when I could, but that wasn't often enough. When I could walk into any bar or liquor store and legally buy anything I wanted, my downhill slide accelerated significantly. By the time I got sober in May of 1995, I was beaten. I had known something was wrong long before—I had first tried AA when I was sixteen, but hadn't been willing to change my life in any way. This time I was ready. The night of my last drunk, I had a vision: I saw myself not far in the future, drinking alone, and dying. I realized I was an alcoholic and called my father, who took me to AA the next day.

I haven't looked back, but it would be a lie to say it has been easy. I was one of very few young people in the town I sobered up in. I got a lot of "I've spilled more than you drank!" and people telling me outright I wouldn't make it. Worst of all, I couldn't get a sponsor. But I stayed sober then for the same reason I stay sober now: I was willing to do absolutely anything to do so. I didn't want to die drunk, and I knew that was what would happen if I didn't get help.

I worked hard the first few years and grew a lot. The Fourth and Fifth Steps helped relieve a lot of the shame that made it feel necessary for me to drink. I began to feel good physically and picked up my university marks so successfully that I was accepted to do graduate work. Things were going well, but I got complacent. My meeting attendance dropped off. I didn't contact many people in AA. I thought I was okay until after I got my master's degree. I found myself working in a foreign country without all the usual support networks, which made complacency that much easier. I managed to find the AA number, and after weeks of excruciating phone tag, I made it to a meeting.

Serious culture shock had awakened me to the danger I was in after a year of slacking off, and I became involved in AA again. I seemed to be doing everything right. I got a sponsor who was serious about the Steps. I went to four meetings a week. I hung out with AA people with good sobriety. Yet, I started being plagued by voices telling me that drinking wasn't as bad as I remembered. I couldn't believe this was happening after five years of sobriety and following all the suggestions. It was then, finally, that I truly accepted in my heart, not just in my head, that I am an alcoholic, now and forever. I realized that in the back of my mind, I'd always believed that because I got sober so young, I would be cured someday. Things I'd heard at meetings but didn't really understand suddenly made sense, especially "My disease wants me back" and "We have a disease that tells us we don't have a disease."

Since then, life has gotten better. I still have thoughts of drinking, but I cherish those passing thoughts because they remind me that I'm not cured and never will be. For me, staying sober depends absolutely on three things: staying involved in AA, remembering where I've come from, and accepting that some part of me will always want to self-destruct. The difference today is that I have choices.

Today, I try to treat others with respect. I try to treat myself with respect, and sometimes that's harder. I try to give back what's been given to me. Next week I celebrate seven years of continuous sobriety. I'm thinking of how miraculous that is and my nose is getting red and my eyes tickly. I've had the opportunity to make amends to several of my family members and friends. I do service work putting on detox meetings and now I'm starting to do public information work at schools. I'm doing graduate work in something I love. And I have a host of real friends today. But all of this is gravy. The real meat is that I've managed to stay sober one day at a time for seven years, no matter what.

C. S.
KINGSTON, ONTARIO

CHAPTER TWO

I EARNED MY SEAT

Young, but no less an alcoholic

"If you are a young alcoholic, older members will see you as being different. It doesn't matter. Don't let them stop you. It's your life, not theirs," writes the author of a letter to Dear Grapevine.

The younger AAs in these pages want you to know they are members of AA—not AA junior, AA lite or Alateen (a valid but different Twelve Step program). And they've earned their seats. Their drunkalogs, such as those featured in the previous Chapter, may be slightly different. The drinking careers may be shorter—at least one member here only drank for three years. Many of the younger crew never took a legal drink. But all of this means nothing except that they were hurting bad enough to stop.

"Alcohol destroyed our lives and we came to AA for help," the author of "All in the Same Boat" writes. "I have had many older members tell me they are proud of me for being so young and getting into the program. I am just as proud of them. Some say, 'You're lucky you're young,' and it's true, I am lucky—not because I am young, but because I have this program to share in fellowship."

That is the prevailing mood throughout this Chapter. These AAs who started young are proud to be in AA (perhaps that's a given because they've chosen to write their stories), and are serious about staying sober. "I am an alcoholic and I am also seventeen—not surprising, because there are many teenage alcoholics," the YPAA author of "Seventeen and Sober" says.

If they happened to "drink less than you spilled"— as the old cliché goes—they may tell you that perhaps if you hadn't spilled so much, you might have gotten here sooner—as the newer cliché goes. The author of "Haven't You Had Enough?" writes: "Today, I know who I am. Very proudly in my meetings I announce that I am an alcoholic."

A TEENAGER'S TEARS OF HOPE
OCTOBER 2002

My name is Jane. I'm an alcoholic, and I'm fifteen years old. I was raised in an alcoholic home. I wasn't the smartest kid nor the prettiest, and all the other kids in school made sure I knew it, every day. So, eventually I turned to alcohol. My older relatives and cousins told me that it was cool, and that I'd be cool if I drank.

I had my very first drink when I was eleven years old. I hated it—the taste, the smell, everything. So, I didn't drink right away. But the year I was fourteen, I wanted to be independent—you know, to take charge and be carefree. And I wanted to be cool. At first, it seemed harmless to have five beers, feel kind of tipsy, and laugh a lot. You see, I had a horrible past, having been molested from the time I was age five to age ten by my own relatives, and then by my older brothers until I was eleven years old. Soon I wasn't drinking once or twice a month; it was every weekend.

That summer, I got a job and a boyfriend who didn't drink. The relationship lasted a month. I lost my boyfriend because I ended up making out with a guy who was twice my age at a party (and who was put into the hospital that morning by my friends). But hey, who cared? I had money, I had friends who were cool, and I was finally cool.

Most weekends were a haze: I'd go to a party, drink, have a good time, and come Sunday, go home, usually with the cops, but not always, and have a great story to tell for days. The things I usually left out were waking up in strange places half-naked, puking all over myself, and finding mysterious bruises and scrapes on my body in the weirdest places.

Soon fall came, and I was a grade behind, but I didn't care as long as I partied on weekends and had a good time. No problems, no worries, no harm done. That's what I thought, until one day when I went to the bathroom. My groin area was itchy, and I noticed an awful smell and a burning sensation. I never told anyone. I studied some information about sexually-transmitted diseases and read in horror the signs and symptoms of genital herpes. I looked at my body—the bumps on my groin area, the bumps on my lips, the discharge in my underwear. I cried for the longest hours of my life when I read that it was incurable. I still had not gone to see a doctor after nine months. Why? Because I was scared of rejection, of dying, of losing all my friends and family.

Guess what came to the rescue? Alcohol and this time, drugs. I started to drink anything, anytime, anywhere, with anybody. I'm fifteen, and every time I went for a drink I was waiting to die. I tried every strategy: getting into cars with drunk drivers, going home with anybody, and eventually trying to commit suicide three times by taking pills, hanging, and cutting myself. No luck. Finally, my mom put me in a treatment center. I came in unwillingly, expecting a bunch of losers who couldn't control their drinking, bums, hookers, crackheads, losers. That wasn't me. I thought I was the complete opposite—cool, clean-cut, with class and style. Wrong. These people were my age, struggling to fight the disease called alcoholism. They looked normal and didn't seem to smell or act funny. So I checked in, planning to party harder when I got out.

I started to have withdrawal shakes, sweating, moodiness, and worst of all, I was probably the most insane person in there. Then the weirdest thing happened. I began to follow the program in treatment, and I went to some AA meetings. I finally cried, not out of anger, guilt, or shame, but with tears of hope that I could survive, not for anybody or anything else, but for me. I graduate this Saturday. I'm very scared.

ANONYMOUS
ONTARIO

ALL IN THE SAME BOAT
FEBRUARY 1987

My name is K—and I am an alcoholic. I went to my first AA meeting when I was fourteen years old, which means nothing except that I have the disease of alcoholism. Now, almost seventeen years old, I have been sober since March of 1984. The length of time sober is really of no importance to me. I am sober today, and that is how I take my program—one day at a time. I feel that quality of sobriety is more important than quantity.

I am writing this mainly with the hope that fellow AA members will relate to it, no matter how old, how young, or how long sober. We are all in the same boat—alcohol destroyed our lives and we came to AA for help.

I drank three years of my life away—three years of living hell. The three years of drinking are not what brought me to AA. The "hell" is what brought me here, just as it is what brings most of us to AA and to a better way of life.

I just finished reading an article in a 1982 Grapevine, in which the writer stated he was worried about dually addicted members taking over AA meetings; he didn't feel he could relate to them. Well, I have friends who are dually addicted in this program and I, too, like other members, sometimes don't relate with their drug usage. But I don't look down on people who are dually addicted. I try to relate and to be a friend in the same way that they help me—by being friends.

To me it doesn't matter how we get into AA (thank God it's here to get into!). It doesn't matter how much, how little, or how long we drank, just as it doesn't matter how old or how young we are when we get here. What really matters is that we didn't control drinking—drinking controlled us.

I have had many older members tell me they are proud of me for being so young and getting into the program. What they don't realize is that I am just as proud of them. Some say, "You're lucky you're young," and it's true, I am lucky—not because I am young, but because I have this program to share in fellowship.

K. H.
OBERLIN, KANSAS

TWENTY-ONE AND IN TROUBLE AGAIN
JULY 2003

There I was, twenty-one years old and in trouble again. It seems kind of odd that I would look at it as being in trouble, since at the time I had been in prison for over five years.

I had spent those years drinking and hiding from all the guilt I felt inside. You can get anything you want in prison, and the things I wanted most were of the mind-altering variety. I had spent those five years going day to day either drinking the "bootleg" alcohol that we used to make or chasing down a half a pint of grain alcohol somewhere. Finally, it caught up with me. I was sitting in the hole for drinking and using, looking at the very real possibilities of having my expected stay lengthened by at least a year, having my mother turned away on visitation day by a prison guard who'd say that, once again, her wayward son had gone and messed things up for himself.

When I was first put in that isolation cell, the only thing I could think to do was send word to one of my "friends" to send me something to "ease my mind." Thankfully, God's will for me that night was not peace of mind. For the first time in my life, while sitting in that small, dark and lonely cell, I realized that every single problem I had ever had in my life was because of the very thing I thought was the solution.

As the weight of a life gone drastically wrong came crashing down on me, I knew that I had to stop drinking or I would never get out of prison. That night, I said the first prayer I had said in many years.

"God, please help me." No promises or demands, no deals to make or bargains to be had, just one alcoholic's desperate plea for help.

I don't think I realized it at the time, but God began to work in my life immediately. The warden of that unit decided that he didn't want to deal with me anymore. I was sent straight from the hole to another unit that was just opening. I spent the next nine months trying to stop on my own. I would be sober for a few weeks at a time only to go on yet another binge.

Then one day I was standing in the hallway, drunk as usual, when another inmate, who was in the program and whom I had known over the years, asked me what I was going to do. This guy was twenty-two years old with a life sentence and knew he probably would never get out of prison, yet every time I saw him he had a smile on his face. I always thought there had to be something wrong with him.

Being my usual self, I said something smart to him. Then he said something that to this day I thank God for. He said that he meant, "What are you going to do with the rest of your life?" For the first time in my life, it dawned on me that I had absolutely no idea what I was going to do. I knew right then and there that I was lost, but I honestly felt that God had sent this guy to talk to me. He ended up becoming my first sponsor.

I began working the Steps and making the meetings. I spent my time working and reading the Big Book (which became my constant companion). By the grace of God and the miracle of the Twelve Steps, I have not had to take a drink since December 18, 1999.

I was sent to another unit once again, but this time for positive reasons. Today, I go out to schools in and around Little Rock, Arkansas, and share my personal experiences with teenagers. I am the chairperson of the Wrightsville AA Group (who, thank God, constantly remind me that I ain't no big deal), and I regularly have the opportunity to attend the area assembly and district meetings. I cannot begin to express the overwhelming love and support that I have received from the members of the Fellowship. My relationship with my family has been restored with love and support that I never could have imagined possible. I have developed a conscious contact with a loving God, as "I understand him." And I am looking at the very real possibility of being released from prison this year.

Today I can honestly say that I know a new freedom and a new happiness. I don't regret my past, nor wish to shut the door on it. I have seen how my experiences can and have benefited others. I comprehend the word serenity and I know peace. And I realize that God is doing for me the things I cannot do myself. I also know that none of these things has come about because of me. The only thing I ever accomplished was getting myself put in prison. I owe each and every day of my sobriety to God, and to you, the Fellowship of Alcoholics Anonymous, especially those of you who carry the message to us AAs in prison.

HOWARD W.
WRIGHTSVILLE, ARKANSAS

YOUNG AND IN PAIN
DEAR GRAPEVINE, JULY 2003

When I came to my first meeting in 1980, I was twenty-three years and eleven months old. Most members of that group were age thirty or older. They tried to treat me like an alcoholic, but I felt their patronizing attitude. A few told me, "If you are not an alcoholic in disgrace, you are in time to stop and save yourself fifteen years of the pain we suffered." But one said, "You are not an alcoholic. Don't waste your time here. Go outside. Find a girlfriend and take her to the movies."

The words of those members were not enough to stop me from attending meetings. I knew, I felt, there was something in the meeting room for me. After ten years of drinking, I was ready to receive help. After suffering an internal pain for years (loneliness, resentment, hate—the relief for which was drinking), I was touched by God's grace and decided to get what those AA members had. I hit bottom in my country, Mexico. I lead my first AA meeting there in 1980. I have not had a single drink since.

If you are a young alcoholic, older members will see you as being different. But it doesn't matter. Don't let them stop you. It's your life, not theirs. Go to meetings, find a sponsor, get into service, until you get what the winners in AA have gotten: a full and sober life.

JOSÉ A.M.
LOS ANGELES, CALIFORNIA

WANTED
MAY 1997

Fourteen years old and two thousand miles from home I realized something wasn't right in my life. I had run away from home two months before so that I'd be able to be "on my own." I found myself in Amarillo, Texas. I'd been running with a gang but now I found myself on the street. I feared the night. I found food in the dumpsters of restaurants until I learned to steal, and stealing became a way of life. It is the way I acquired my booze, my food, my cigarettes, and my clothing. I lived in the fear that someday I'd be caught. Sometimes I got sick to my stomach just thinking about it. It occurred to me that perhaps my life wasn't normal, but the thought would soon pass. This was life as I knew it.

I didn't dream of the day that I'd be a success in a career. Instead I wanted to go back to the time when drinking was fun, when I could sneak out of the house and return late at night, when drinking didn't bring me pain. I didn't want to be alone anymore. I wanted a friend again.

In the fall of that year I was placed in a facility for teenagers with social problems. It was an intense treatment. Most of those with me were convicted criminals. Though I'd also been guilty of crimes, I'd never been caught. The facility was safe and I liked it there. After three and a half months, they released me with the explanation that they were unable to help me. I was diagnosed an alcoholic and AA was strongly suggested.

At the first meeting I attended, I learned of the love that AAs have for each other. I was made to feel welcome. Unlike other organizations, there were no dues or initiation fees. In fact, I was told not to contribute until I'd been there six weeks. AA was different from anything I'd ever heard of. I was wanted.

It has been over seven years since I took a drink. Life hasn't been all smooth sailing, but because of AA, I no longer have to live in fear. I sleep at night. I have a new relationship with my Creator. I have a purpose in life.

SHANE L.
MANKATO, MINNESOTA

A FRESH INTRODUCTION TO HELL
JULY 1998

started drinking when I was eleven years old. My grandpa was drinking beer and he asked me if I wanted a sip. I said yes. My sip was finishing off the bottle, and then drinking quite a few more. I hated the taste of beer and despised the smell, but when the effects hit me, I was in love. My whole body burned with a numbing fire. I could stand on top of the world with alcohol. All my problems went away.

Right off I was an everyday drinker. I stole from my friends' parents, hung out at slop houses, and went to parties. None of the people I went to school with had any clue what I was doing. But I was hooked.

For a year, no one knew that I was drinking almost all the time. At twelve years old, I had my first experience with drugs and I got that high feeling again—the feeling that I could stand on top of the world. I was popular, beautiful, and bulletproof. My journey with drugs progressed rapidly with the aid of my alcoholism.

It was fun for a time. The parties were good, the friends were good, life seemed good. But the fun didn't last. It became harder to get the things I needed from people. School authorities didn't like my habits or my attitudes, so I was kicked out of every school I went to.

My parents were baffled. They didn't know that I was drinking and drugging; they thought I was going through a rebellious phase. I didn't care what they thought as long as they didn't know the truth.

I didn't know the truth either—that I had a problem that was steadily getting worse. I started prostituting for drugs, and it ripped me up inside. Getting out of bed every morning was a fresh introduction to hell.

In January 1996, I ran away from home. I was sleeping on curbs in the Utah winter. I couldn't control my craving for alcohol. I had reached my bottom.

Two weeks later, my parents found me. They took me to an adolescent psychiatric ward where I made an alcohol inventory and got a Big Book that I read cover to cover. But when I got out of treatment, I didn't know where to go and I started drinking again. My relapse lasted a little over three weeks. I woke up one morning, looked in the mirror and started to cry. I was fourteen, weighed eighty-five pounds, had stringy hair and dead eyes lined with fatigue. That person in the mirror scared me; I didn't want it to be me. I needed help.

I called my psych ward and my counselor gave me the number of an AA central office. I took it. I felt hope resurfacing in my life for the first time in years.

I didn't call for another week. I was scared; I wasn't sure what I would say. I stayed dry for that week, but I was miserable. Finally, that misery became too much to bear. I picked up the phone and called.

A really nice lady answered. She took my name and number and told me that someone would get back to me as soon as possible. Someone did. That person took me to my first meeting.

I don't remember a whole lot that was said at that meeting, but there was a feeling of happiness and peace in that room and it affected me.

I started going to meetings every day. I got a sponsor. I began to work the Steps. I got into lots of service work. Surprisingly enough, my life began to change for the better. I found a Higher Power of my own understanding.

Now I'm sixteen years old, and I'm coming up on two years of sobriety. I'd love to tell you that life has been easy and sweet since I got sober, but some days I have to really work to keep my sanity. But I have a program for living that makes it much easier.

Life is better today. I have a support group of friends who have stuck with me in sobriety. I feel things now, and I don't mind feeling them. I have a relationship with a guy in the Fellowship, and he helps me in ways I can't describe.

Only one thing really helps me: I try to listen to the suggestions and the experiences. "Keep Coming Back" also helps. This program isn't for those who need it; it's for those who want it. I'm just glad I wanted it badly enough.

BREANNE M.
SALT LAKE CITY, UTAH

HOW BAD IS BAD ENOUGH?
DEAR GRAPEVINE, OCTOBER 2003

I am a nineteen-year-old alcoholic. My sobriety date is February 11, 2003. Since I have been coming to meetings, I have heard things like "It's good that you came to AA before anything bad happened to you." Statements like these make me feel inferior. It's like saying my alcoholic career was a breeze. I may not have been drinking as long as most AAs, but don't tell me that I haven't experienced bottom. Last year, I went to six rehabs (three inpatient, three outpatient), and a halfway house, and at one point, I was in a coma. Yet I still drank. After my last detox experience, I gave up the fight and surrendered to God. I believe that God brings us into the rooms of

Alcoholics Anonymous at the right time. If we pick up once again, we weren't ready. I just hope I can be of service to young people and other alcoholics.

MIKE C.
PITTSBURGH, PENNSYLVANIA

HAVEN'T YOU HAD ENOUGH?
AUGUST 1999

As I sat in my chair and looked around the room, I thought to myself that there was no way I belonged with these people. So what if I drank a little more than my friends? An alcoholic I was not. I was too young.

I started drinking at the age of eleven. When I drank, I became funny and beautiful, and it seemed to me I had friends. But somewhere along the way I crossed an invisible line, and drinking was no longer something I could choose. My friends had begun to say, "Haven't you had enough?" But as drunk as I was, I had just started.

My self-esteem vanished. I was no one. Only when a man said I was beautiful, did I even think, Maybe I'm all right.

I hated the sight of what I'd become. I started to isolate. I became suicidal. My parents, not knowing that I was drinking, didn't know what to do with a depressed teenager.

Then I found tequila, and during my last year of drinking, I never drew a sober breath. I drank to a point of no friends and no self-worth. No one could trust me, not even my parents. The next day, I was in a thirty-day treatment program. That day, sobriety began. It was March 21, 1988. I was thirteen years old.

Today, I know who I am. Very proudly in my meetings I announce that I am an alcoholic. I pray daily, even just to ask my Higher Power (whom I choose to call God) to walk with me that day. He has never left me, even when I left him. I'm active in AA—shaking hands, chairing meetings, coffee duty, reading, and sharing my experience, strength, and hope. I try to live the Twelve Steps of AA. I've found that they apply to my every situation in life since I still have to learn to live life on life's terms

Every one of us in AA is a miracle. The gratitude I have is just to be breathing today. I was so close to dying. And although I have a lot of "yets" out there, I have true friends who love me. All I need to do is call them and go to meetings, work my program, and for today the "yets" won't come.

So I write this to thank all of you for keeping the AA program strong and giving me a chance to continue my sobriety today.

A.C.B.
RALEIGH, NORTH CAROLINA

REACHING TEENS
DEAR GRAPEVINE, FEBRUARY 2001

have been sober for two months. I just got out of juvenile detention. I am fourteen and have been drinking for five years.

No, I am not lying. My family life permitted me to do such things. I was put in juvenile detention after I was arrested for escaping from a treatment center. Now I am in a long-term treatment house for teenage girls. It's a very good place.

I am just writing to say that young people are serious about quitting. I have been around a lot of runaways who were attempting to quit but couldn't without some sort of positive motivation like I have found in AA. I think that you would be able to reach out to younger people nationwide with a teen Grapevine and/or youth oriented AA groups. It would be inspiration for people who someday will be either drunks or honest, trustworthy citizens who can make America proud.

MANDIE W.
BELLINGHAM, WASHINGTON

SEVENTEEN AND SOBER
JANUARY 1978

I am an alcoholic and I am also seventeen—not surprising, because there are many teenage alcoholics. Half of them don't even know they have a problem. I'm one of the lucky ones; I found out in time.

I have been drinking since I was eight. Physically, it didn't take its toll until the last three years. But mentally, it affected me from the very first drink I picked up.

My story is a common one. I drank because I had problems—in other words, to cop out. I wasn't very happy at home. Although I was loved, I didn't feel wanted. The bottle was my friend. It helped me cope.

As the years passed by and my drinking progressed, I became obsessed with alcohol. I needed it to do just about everything. At about the age of twelve, I went from scotch on weekends to drinking beer with my friends. They had discovered drinking, and now I didn't have to drink alone any more. We would walk up to the deli and get a couple of quarts apiece. But I was never satisfied with just two quarts. This was when I suspected something was wrong.

By this time, it had really caught up with me. I missed days from school, mostly Mondays and Fridays. No longer did I drink only on weekends. I drank on weekdays, too. I drank in the morning to calm my nerves and steady my shaking hands. Then the resentments and the fears set in.

At fourteen, I was contemplating suicide. I couldn't find any reason to live. I hadn't even begun to live, and I wanted to die. It was a vicious cycle of morning sickness and shaking and night drinking. Drinking wasn't fun any more. I didn't enjoy the high as I used to. By now, I couldn't function without alcohol. I had lost everything—my self-respect and my will to live. I was embarrassing my family, and no longer was I the life of the party. I was a drunk. I knew what I was doing was wrong. But what was I going to do? I would try anything to stop.

I knew someone in AA and decided to try it. With no idea of what to expect, I went to my first meeting on January 16, 1976. I was afraid to talk. If anyone came near me, I started to shake. Through my sponsor and my Higher Power, I made it—but not right away. It took me a couple of months. Now, I know why. It was because I didn't open up. I wouldn't let anyone help me. Then I surrendered. It was the most important thing I had ever done. I just let go and let God.

The difference since I've been in AA is amazing. Before, I kept everything to myself, because I didn't think I needed anyone. I had forgotten how to smile, and laughing was a thing of the past. But since I've been in the program, it has helped me more than I can say. I'm learning to smile and laugh again, and I've even gotten back some of my self-respect. The friends I have in AA are the best friends I'll ever have. I still have problems, but AA has taught me how to handle them and not run from them. I am very grateful to AA for my new life. I believe God has given me a second chance. So I will carry the AA message to anyone who needs and wants it.

ANONYMOUS
RICHMOND, NEW YORK

CHAPTER THREE

THE NEXT GENERATION

Growing up around AA is no guarantee against alcoholism

"I grew up knowing all the program's slogans and philosophy. But that didn't stop me from feeling different and very alone," writes the author of "Blessed With the Memory of My Pain."

One AA's father had joined the Fellowship, but was sober on and off. Another resented her mother because of her drinking, and then resented AA after her mother got sober. A third was raised by two sets of parents and stepparents who were active alcoholics. On the flip side, one young person grew up a house that was "the local detox center" and the AA social hub for two recovering parents. These children of alcoholics never expected to become alcoholics themselves, and some had very intimate knowledge of the workings of the program.

"My dad had been a member for over eighteen years, and my mom was an Al-Anon member. I remember being five years old, running around the kitchen as the coffeepot rumbled and the air filled with cigarette smoke. I never dreamed that one day I would be drinking coffee as a member of the group," writes one author.

Sometimes the parents' disease helps the alcoholic find the program sooner. They realize, from their parents' example, what they are becoming. Other times the parent takes the younger alcoholic to a meeting, detox or treatment center. The parents' peers may become the younger AA's mentors. Gradually, the YPAA finds his own path of recovery. "I found out I had to work my program my way, for me, or it just doesn't work. I'm thankful that my family lets me work my program the best way I can, even if I make mistakes," a member wrote in 1980.

And the author of "My Grandma's Gift" directly credits her grandmother's tough attitude with her own sobriety. "Had it not been for my grandma coming before me, I do not know if I would have thought to join AA. I believe she saved me years of suffering."

A PROGRAM BABY
NOVEMBER 1994

When I was born in 1966, my dad was a member of AA and my mom was attending Al-Anon, so that makes me a "program baby." While my father did get periods of sobriety, he unfortunately did not get long-term, continuous sobriety. Because of this I saw the damage an active alcoholic can cause.

Some might think that since I grew up seeing lots of booze-related troubles, I would never have drunk. Unfortunately, this was not the case. I started drinking around my eighteenth birthday and looking back on it, I was drinking antisocially from the very start. My early drinking often took place in deserted parks, or behind a hockey arena. Typically, it involved drinking beer or straight liquor as fast as possible to just get drunk. I drank like this before high school dances and parties, but often there was no special occasion, other than the fact it was Friday night.

I had my first blackout on my third drinking spree, when I and two friends split a bottle of rum. I found out the next morning that I had been violent, had been shouting and running in the streets, and had fallen over a concrete retaining wall and cut open my elbow. Needless to say this incident caused a major racket at home and I remember my father (sober at the time) saying something like, "What are you doing? Can't you see what it's done to me?" My dad passed away about two weeks after my foray. However, neither the death of my father nor the previous incident stopped me from drinking. I kept drinking for six years, until the age of twenty-four. I did try one AA meeting in 1987 or 1988 after a particularly bad night, but I wasn't ready and didn't stay around.

My drinking was generally characterized by unpredictability. I could not predict how much I would drink, what my behavior would be, where I would end up, or whether or not I would have a blackout. There were nights when I could drink a lot and be fairly social, and not have a blackout. There were other times when I would drink a relatively small amount and black out or do something embarrassing. Then there were the times when I would go somewhere and plan to have two or three, and end up loaded! For example, I had a really bad night in January 1990. I was in the second semester of a university program and was invited to a house party thrown by one of my professors. I brought a half-dozen beers with me and planned on having "a few" and socializing. Yeah, right. Around 2 AM or so, I was sitting at my host's kitchen table with two buddies drinking a mixture of cooking sherry and beer. I can remember most of the party, up until shortly after the host threw us out, at around 2:30 AM, I think. I left the party with an acquaintance to walk downtown for pizza. I blacked out shortly after leaving the party and my recollections of the rest of the evening are sketchy at best. Unfortunately, my memories of the next morning are all too vivid. I remember the awful headache, my parchment dry throat, and worst of all, my racing mind. What happened? What time did I get home? Had I done something that would get me kicked out of university? Were the police looking for me?

I do not want to forget the period from January to May 1990. I went through hell. Crazy as it might seem, I drank two or three times after that "party"; however, each time it was one or two beers. The last beer I had was around St. Patrick's Day 1990. The next couple of months were really rough. I was trying to complete graduate course work and keep my sanity. I was paranoid, disoriented, and isolated. Six years of blackouts had really forced me to avoid a lot of people due to fear and shame.

I began seeing a psychiatrist in May 1990, and she used to say things to me like, "That sounds like something an alcoholic would say." Finally, after about three months of talking to this woman I went to an AA meeting. By luck the meeting I went to was the West End Group, which meets on Mundy Pond Road in St. John's. At this meeting were many people who knew my dad and mom and many fine people who were very helpful to me. After three or four months of attending meetings, I joined the West End Group and slowly began to get involved. Today I am twenty-eight years old, have finished my university program, have found work, am dry four years, and am GSR (general service representative) for my group. I consider myself an AA miracle.

Over my relatively short time in AA I think I've learned a little about the first drink. For example, I know that it only takes one drink to get me started again. I might get away with drinking for a week, a month, or six months, but sooner or later one drink is going to lead me to a lot more, and a blackout, and God knows what else. I have to do my best to avoid one drink, one day at a time. I do this by attending meetings, by staying active in my group, and by asking my Higher Power for help at the start of the day. From John D. (who is sober thirty years and who drank with my dad) I have learned that I am responsible for the first drink. I am a self-confessed alcoholic and am a potential menace when drinking. Therefore, I have to avoid one drink at all costs. Consider a forest fire and how a single match or a single cigarette butt can start a blaze that destroys a vast amount of land. Similarly, one drink is capable of "starting a fire" that can certainly destroy me and hurt people around me. I get my "fire insurance" one day at a time by staying close to my home group and my Higher Power.

I often think of my dad and how different things might have been had he avoided one drink and gotten long-term sobriety. Of course, we cannot change the past, and I guess that things happen as they must. The new life I'm building for myself hinges upon me not taking one drink, for just one day. It is a simple but at times difficult plan to follow. Life can be hard, but no matter what comes up in the run of a day, I have to remember that I cannot pick up a drink. As long as I can avoid one drink, I'll be okay. Things might not always go exactly as I might like, but I will be okay.

DARRIN M.
ST. JOHN'S, NEWFOUNDLAND

HEADS UP
OCTOBER 1998

My name is Alison and I'm an alcoholic. When I came to Alcoholics Anonymous, I was a twenty-one-year-old little girl, full of fear and loneliness. As far back as I can remember, I was shy and couldn't talk to anyone. I never thought I was good enough, pretty enough, smart enough. I never held my head up when I walked or even when I talked with anyone. All this was before I picked up my first drink. That was another thing—I was never going to drink. I was not going to be like my mother. I hated her for her drinking and blamed her for everything I went through in life. I never wanted anyone to hate me like I hated her. When I was five years old, my mom got sober in AA, and then besides hating her, I hated AA for taking my mother away from me. My whole life was definitely about blame.

From the first time I drank, I blacked out. I was irresponsible, I got away with it, and I wanted more! I was eleven years old. Alcohol was my way out of shyness; it allowed me to make friends and be cool. By the age of fourteen, I was drinking almost every day. By this time, I had to stay close to home because of fear. But I was even petrified of my own bedroom windows and actually blocked them with cardboard boxes and painted them black so no one could see in and I couldn't see out. I used to crawl through my house, thinking "they" would see me. Who knows who "they" were. I couldn't do anything alone, like go to a store, call someone up, or go to school. Alcohol was not helping my shyness anymore.

When I was fifteen, I overdosed on alcohol. I drank so much beer, wine, and vodka that my BAC (blood alcohol level) was .375 (.4 is dead). That produced a pause in my drinking, but not even a year later, it started all over again. Now I was drinking sips of beer, because I'd decided I was never drinking hard liquor again. But almost every time I drank, I blacked out. Alcohol became more important to me than friends or school. I didn't care who I hurt, as long as I got what I wanted. I didn't want to remember, feel, or know anything. I drank to oblivion.

By the age of twenty, I had no friends and had lost the ability to stay at home and do what I wanted without feeling shame and guilt. My family disowned me, and I was living wherever I could sleep. I had lost all respect for myself. On October 19, 1995, I spent my twenty-first birthday in a public defender's office, because the day before that I'd been arrested for stealing checks from my grandmother. As I was leaving that office that morning, I was, as usual, walking with my head down, and a woman staff member said to me, "You know, you don't have to walk with your head down anymore." My first thought was that she was crazy. I had no clue what she was talking about.

During the next month, I tried hard not to drink, but I had to. On November 14, I went into rehab and admitted I was an alcoholic and believed it in my heart. I wanted to do anything to never go back to where I was. After completing rehab, I went directly into an intensive outpatient program. I didn't want AA because that was my mother's life and I didn't want it to be part of mine. However, the outpatient program was ending, and I had nowhere to go again. I knew I'd drink if I didn't continue to get help, so I called a friend and started to attend AA meetings. I got a sponsor and joined a home group. By working the Steps into my life, one day at a time, with the help of God and a sponsor, I now have hope and a chance at being happy, joyous, and free. From the time I got a sponsor she told me that I was a woman of honor and dignity. Today I feel it. As it says in the Big Book: "As God's people, we stand on our feet; we don't crawl before anyone."

I'm a couple of months short of two years of sobriety. Today, I walk with my head up high, and I understand what that woman was talking about.

ALISON B.
STONY POINT, NEW YORK

WHEN I WAS SIXTEEN, I WAS READY
JANUARY 1978

came into the program of AA when I was sixteen years old, and believe me, I was ready. My drinking had started some ten years before, at the age of six. My pilling had started at the age of nine. So you see, I'd had ample time to become an alcoholic.

Both of my real parents were (and still are, of course) alcoholics. I was brought up in this environment and I swore to myself that I would never become whatever they were. I had three stepparents who also were alcoholics, and I couldn't believe that there was any other kind of life.

From as far back as I can remember, I felt that I was not as good as anyone else. The other kids had nice clothes and looked as though they couldn't be happier, while I stayed in the background, wishing that I could be like them. I felt fat and ugly and clumsy as an ox. So when I found what alcohol could do for me, you can understand why I had found my heaven.

I went back and forth between my parents after their divorce. Finally, when I was nine, my father remarried again, and we supposedly had a home. My new stepmother and I did not get along at all. I hated her and the whole world. My life was filled with hate and self-pity. I found out that if you took a nice-size amount of aspirins or other home remedies, you could feel different. You weren't so ugly or fat or anything else that you didn't want to be. I read to escape reality and imagined myself in the characters' place. I dreamed and lived in a world of my own, and no one else could come in.

Even though my mother stayed drunk and often abused us, I never hated her. For some strange reason, I knew she was sick. I worshipped her and put her on a pedestal. She was my idol. I wanted for thirteen years to live with her, and always my father would say no.

People were just watching to see if I would turn out like my mother.

When I reached thirteen, all hell broke loose. Rebellion was my way of life. Hate, bitterness, self-pity, and resentments controlled my entire being. I wanted everyone else to hurt like I did, and I therefore caused a lot of pain in other peoples' lives. I ran away from home, was suspended from school, carried whiskey in my purse in a mouthwash bottle, and got soused to the gills in other peoples' houses. Escape! Relief! All I wanted was out. I'd had suicidal tendencies since I was nine. Now, I was trying to carry them out, wanting to die but also afraid to die.

My parents thought I didn't mean to be this way, so they took me to a headshrinker. I lied, conned, and everything else, so this did no good. Teachers would try to tell me that I was a nice girl and that I shouldn't be hanging around with these kids who stayed in trouble. My shrink gave me tranquilizers, and I had found my heaven again.

I became engaged to my Sunday-school teacher, so that I could be good, and that didn't work; I joined the church, and that didn't work. Dear God, nothing worked! I went through another engagement, and finally, three months after I turned sixteen, I hit bottom, the lowest pits of despair. I was a nervous wreck and a walking zombie. I had been in the hospital for "nerves" some time before that. I couldn't take any more. I thought, Well, this time I am really going to kill myself and do it right.

But God stepped in and gave me a thought: Call Mother. So I called her and said, "What can I do to come live with you?"

She said, "Pray."

Brother! I thought. Why ask God for something when he has let all this happen to me? How could he be the good and almighty God that everyone said he was? But I thought, What have I got to lose? For the first time in my life, I prayed. I said, "God, if you want me to live with my mother, give me the words to say."

When the opportunity arose, I went to my father and said, "Daddy, can I talk to you?" For the first time, he said yes. I told him I couldn't live with him any longer and that I wanted to live with my mother.

For the first time in my life, I saw my father cry. This man who had no feeling except for the bottle was crying. He told me that he was not giving me permission, but he wasn't going to stop me. So I got on the bus with the feeling that everything was going to be all right. I wouldn't have to pill or drink any more, I thought. I even gave a poor man on the bus a supply of pills.

This didn't last very long. Less than two weeks later, I went on a week's bender. During this time, I became engaged to a man I had known for a week. He was headed for Vietnam. He said those three little magic words that I craved hearing so much: "I love you."

I realized then, with the help of my mother and stepfather, that I had a problem. They are both in AA, and I wanted help so desperately that I tried AA. But the fears were still there. I had to go to a new school with new people, and I couldn't face all those people on my own, so I went to the medicine cabinet and reached for the mouthwash. Drinking it gave me courage at first, but then it did nothing but make me sick.

Finally, with the help of two wonderful, understanding parents, I came into the program of AA, and I tried to get what these people had. It hasn't been easy, but I've slowly found what living really is. Now, I can hold up my head and mix with people and not be afraid of what they are thinking of me. I am finding an inner peace that I have never known before. I don't have to rely on sex to know that I am loved. I am accepted as an alcoholic, even though I am quite young. I'm learning to like myself and love and accept love. This is truly a miracle.

And now, with almost a year and a half of sobriety, I will soon be eighteen. People often say, "What a horrible thing to happen to one so young!" But I am not sorry. I am glad for everything that has happened to me. I have found a way of life that I wouldn't trade for anything in the world. I can honestly say I am proud to be an alcoholic. God has found a purpose for me, and I am truly trying to fulfill this purpose—to carry the message to other sick alcoholics and say I understand, to show them what my Higher Power has done for me, and to tell them that through AA they can find happiness, serenity, and a way to arrest this disease called alcoholism.

I thank God every day for this wonderful program, and I also pray that out there there may be some young person who has a problem and will read this and realize there is hope.

J. I.
MAGNOLIA, ARKANSAS

SECOND-GENERATION AA
DEAR GRAPEVINE, OCTOBER 1980

I just had to write this letter of appreciation to AA. I wasn't always this thankful for the program. I was raised in or around AA, as I have a parent in the program since before I was born. I resented AA for taking my family from me. I didn't understand their need for meetings, but now I do.

I put off coming to AA myself, even though I needed help. I didn't want to embarrass my dad. Well, I found out that the people accepted me for what I was—a person who needed help.

Since joining the program eight months ago, I find I am fortunate—there are other people with fathers and mothers in AA. What a way to share! This has helped me to learn more about my illness and to accept it.

I can remember reading the Grapevine when I was a child, but the only thing I read was Victor E. Now, I read anything and everything about AA and enjoy it.

One more note: I found out I had to work my program my way, for me, or it just doesn't work. I'm thankful that my family lets me work my program the best way I can, even if I make mistakes. I am thankful I no longer put AA down like I did as a child. It has become my way of life, and a good one.

T. J.
BELLEVILLE, ILLINOIS

BLESSED WITH THE MEMORY OF MY PAIN
JANUARY 1996

When I was born, my father was a full-blown alcoholic and my mother was an untreated Al-Anon. However, when I was two, my father hit bottom and found the Fellowship of AA, and not long after, my mother found Al-Anon. My house often turned into the local detox center, since the only treatment facility in the area had a rule that drunks had to be dry for at least twenty-four hours before they could enter treatment.

So I grew up knowing all the program's slogans and philosophy. But that didn't stop me from feeling different and very alone. Since I was the middle kid (of three), my folks took pains to make sure I wasn't left out or lost as many middle kids are. I thought they were just trying to be nice to me because I wasn't as good as my brother and sister.

By the time I turned twelve, my brother had been in Alateen for over two years. My folks saw how it had helped him and told me I had to go to my first meeting. Anything after that would be my choice.

When I went to my first Alateen meeting I was petrified. There were thirty teenagers crowded into this room that was designed to fit twenty. I knew some of the others from AA functions but most were strangers and much older—seventeen and eighteen years old. I kept my eyes down and my mouth shut and told my parents it was fun because I knew that's what they wanted to hear. I continued to go to Alateen for a number of reasons—I kind of enjoyed it, it made my folks happy, and there were cute girls. As time went on, however, I came to be really miserable. I knew all the literature by heart but didn't know how to work the program with my heart. I was quick to give the best advice but didn't feel I really belonged and couldn't bring any of my problems to the group.

But I found other ways to help me deal with my problems—

alcohol and drugs. At the same time I was becoming quite a popular guy around school (though I never could figure out why). I was elected president of the school and hated every minute of it. I would have quit but I didn't know if I could and still have people like me.

After dating a real neat gal for a couple of years we were engaged. She was going to make me happy. She was a real early bird, which helped me hide my drinking. After I took her home, I'd go out and get wasted and she never knew.

I was not exactly happy at this point in my life and I started to look for reasons why. I was twenty years old and still living with my parents so that had to be it. I needed my freedom. I moved out. It didn't help. That just gave me more free time to experiment with drugs, and I took to it with a passion. My girlfriend wasn't making me happy, so I broke up with her. That didn't help either. Now I was lonely, guilty, and drunk. Finally I found what the problem was—I was a young progressive thinker in a slow old southern city. I needed real freedom, so I moved.

That was a disaster. Away from those who knew me, I went wild. I spent eighteen months drinking all the time and taking all the drugs I could find, buy, or borrow. I wound up living alone with no food, furniture, money, or hope. I was so sick that I tried to commit suicide. Thank God that didn't work.

I was out of options, and I finally returned to my parents' home. My mother asked if my problems might be related to "chemicals" and I honestly didn't think so. I was just depressed. I went to a psychiatrist to help me get out of this depression and after talking for a while he asked me if I drank. Of course I drank, but not that much. In fact I couldn't remember the last time I had gotten drunk. He suggested that it might be a good idea for me not to drink because I had the classic symptoms for alcoholism. That was a mighty and confusing blow.

While asking myself if it could be true that I was an alcoholic, I went to a friend's Fourth of July party. A strange thing happened there. I kept putting my empty beer bottles down in one place instead of throwing them in the garbage can. When I finished my eighth beer in an hour, I realized I was just as sober as when I started. I had no idea that that was my last drink.

I decided it was a good idea for me to go back to Al-Anon (it had been two years). I knew where a meeting was and I made it a point to be there. I got to the church right as the meeting was about to start and headed for the room with the lights on and in I went. Just as I sat down someone started reading the Preamble and then "How It Works." I had gone to the AA meeting! I was stunned but I knew that this could be no accident. I just thought, Okay, God, you put me here so I'll listen. Wonder of wonders, I could identify with the people there.

I'm now almost four years sober—one day at a time. Things haven't been all roses but they are certainly not comparable to the way they were. God has blessed me with a vivid memory of my pain, which has helped me on many occasions when the thought of escaping popped into my head.

DAN R.
KENNER, LOUISIANA

RIPPED JEANS AND THREADBARE HIGH-TOPS
JUNE 1999

I was reading the December 1998 issue of the Grapevine when I saw a notice requesting personal stories of old-timers and young people. Well, I'm not an old-timer and I'm not a young person anymore, but I was once young and God willing will one day be an old-timer. So with this in mind, I've decided to submit my story to the Grapevine.

My name is Gina and I'm an alcoholic. Eleven years ago at the age of sixteen, I couldn't say these words. It was October 1986, and I was sitting in my first AA meeting. My dad had been a member for over eighteen years, and my mom was an Al-Anon member. I remember being five years old, running around the kitchen as the coffeepot rumbled and the air filled with cigarette smoke. AA coffee parties were a regular thing as I grew up. I never dreamed that one day I would be drinking coffee as a member of the group.

I took my first drink at age thirteen. This is also the first time I got drunk. Alcohol took away all my problems. It made me smarter, better looking, stronger, and more outgoing. I was (or thought I was) a super-teen until I turned sixteen. I was just released from the drunk tank, had no place to go, lost my job, got kicked out of school, and had no friends to turn to. To top everything off, I was two months pregnant. Some mother I'd be, I thought, as I looked at my ripped jeans and threadbare high-tops.

With my head down, I went to my mom and dad. That cold night in October, we went to an AA meeting. I have to be honest when I tell this part: I wish I could say my whole life changed from this day on; it didn't. Living a life of sobriety didn't come easy. Every weekend was a struggle. I'm not proud to admit it, but I did have a slip that lasted three months. I gave birth to a beautiful girl. She helped open my eyes to the destructive lifestyle I was living. I went back to AA in March of 1987 at the age of seventeen.

Today, my eleven-year-old daughter runs around the kitchen during our coffee parties. My husband and I are both AA members today. I still have rough days, but I know where to go when these days crop up—our AA clubroom. I believe anyone can be helped if they have an honest desire to stop drinking. I'm living proof.

GINA L.
THE PAS, MANITOBA

ADDICTED TO EXCITEMENT
JULY 1994

When I was in high school, Fridays were really exciting—the beginning of the weekend! A surge of energy ran through my body: it was party time. On the outside, I'd been "good" all week, while on the inside I either was remorseful about my drunken behavior the weekend before (having done things I normally wouldn't have done sober), or secretly longing for the coming weekend when I could have more fun. The remorse had usually subsided by Thursday, so by Friday I was primed.

My standard question was: "Where are the good parties?" The secret questions that I dared not speak aloud were: "How can I get more beer? How can I stay out later without blowing my good-girl cover?" I didn't hang around people my age on the weekends (that might ruin my reputation). Mostly the people I partied with were in their mid-twenties. They purchased more alcohol, so we never ran out.

My fear forced me to play it semi-cool. I needed to prevent my (now recovering) parents from catching on that all signs of a drinking problem were positive. I had direct experience with alcoholism both through my parents' drinking and from Alateen. I knew the rules of how not to become an alcoholic: don't drink alone (I didn't think it counted when I continued to drink after everyone else had quit for the night), don't let your grades drop (whew, I still had that aced), and don't black out. (Was that a blackout when I was twelve? I walked into the kitchen and the next thing I knew, my cousins were pulling me away from broken glass scattered all over the floor. No, blackouts last hours, days even. It must not have been a real blackout.)

Well, let's not analyze my drinking any longer; let's get back to the excitement of going out! I would think to myself. I never understood why my "straight" friends didn't like getting drunk. They wouldn't even go out with me, except one friend, and she couldn't even drink one wine cooler; I had to finish it off for her. My "best" friend on the other hand really knew how to party. She knew where the good parties took place: where the alcohol was plentiful and where the "real men" hung out. Such excitement! The flirtation ... the choosing ... the capture. This was almost as exciting as the drunken high. The alcohol made me forget that they used me ... and I used them.

Well, it's five-and-a-half years later. I live now in Golden, twenty miles south of the University of Colorado in Boulder. I've been at this college thing since 1987—sober. I used to say that I didn't know what happened, that I just accidentally quit drinking. It sure wasn't my plan, but I'm grateful that it was somebody's plan. Yes, once in a while I feel like I'm missing out. My denial creeps in and presents me with a glimmering of hope that I could drink for a few more years (maybe just till I finish college) and then quit. That occurs when I forget the true story of my drinking. Then I remember what my sponsor said when I read her my Fourth Step. She said, "Oh my, you've packed quite a lot into a short amount of time. I wish I could have packed that much in. I tried!" And we laughed.

Today I don't spend my Friday afternoons outlining my eyes perfectly, spraying my curled hair, and finding the right sweater to match my tight jeans. I don't spend my Friday nights chugging anything I can get my hands on. (I never understood why they took the time to make Fuzzy Navels and those other fancy drinks; just give me the vodka!) I don't practice my breathing by smoking a pack of cigarettes. I don't even send out those flirtatious glances. I don't blow off my friends and end up with some guy, and I don't spend the early hours of Saturday morning regurgitating what I consumed several hours earlier.

So what am I doing tonight? Writing a journal entry instead of "getting ready." Going to a meeting rather than going to a party. Showing my true self rather than a convenient mask.

Before, I arranged my outsides, and now I prepare my insides. In the past, I looked for that exciting high. Now I receive a spiritual energy which lasts much longer. I'm still left with myself the next day, but now I like that self. Now my life is real. I am present. I take responsibility for my life. Today I honor and love that scared, depressed teenager who thought she had to live like that. She didn't know any other way. When I tell my story, I acknowledge her strength and her pain, and we heal.

KIMBERLY M.
GOLDEN, COLORADO

MY GRANDMOTHER'S GIFT
FEBRUARY 2009

The funny thing about coming from a family with a history of alcoholism is that, sooner or later, someone will have enough pain and find AA. I am so fortunate that my grandmother came before me.

My grandma, Charlotte, got sober on May 10, 1972. I was born May 12, two days later. She had to come help my parents after my birth. I guess I helped her stay sober that day in her early sobriety. It was a rainy day in May, and she wanted a drink so badly she could not stop thinking about it on the four-hour trip. She had not told her family that she had joined AA, so she knew that no one would question her when she asked for a drink. When she got to our house, the first thing my mother did was ask her if she wanted a drink. Without thought, what came out of her mouth was, "I want a soda." She knew that there was no way she could care for my two brothers if she were drinking, so she did not pick up a drink that day or for the next few days.

Growing up, I never thought one way or the other about my grandma's drinking or lack thereof. It was a non-issue, since she did not drink. Around puberty, I found out she was an alcoholic. I remember hearing this and going back to my cousin's room and laughing. I could not believe it. My grandma was one of the most prim and proper women I had ever known. She ironed handkerchiefs and folded plastic grocery bags—she was the furthest thing from an alcoholic.

Shortly after that, I started getting drunk. I won't say that I started drinking; I never have had one drink in my life. I have always been a drunk. I use to joke that when my grandma got sober her alcoholism jumped to me—that I was born with a beer in one hand and a joint in the other.

As my drinking got worse, so did my attitude. I did not care about anything except where my next escape would come from. My parents were really worried about me, but had no idea what was wrong.

At one point my grandma told my mom, "Kids don't get that way drinking cherry pop." I could never fool my grandma. The only time she confronted me was when I was drunk at a family party and had a major temper tantrum. I wish I could remember what she said. All I remember was being completely blown away that this sweet, prim and proper woman was wiping the floor with me. She knew exactly what I was, even though I was not willing to accept it yet.

I did decide after our talk that marijuana was my problem, so I quit it—and then just drank more. A month after that talk, I ran away from home. When I came back, I threatened to commit suicide and was thrown into a psychiatric ward. Within a couple of weeks, I came to realize that my problem was not my family, teachers, shrinks, friends, acquaintances, or any other real or imagined person against me. I finally accepted that alcohol was my problem. I also knew that AA could help me, because it had helped my grandma.

No one thought I could stay sober because I was only sixteen years old. Newly in AA, I decided to stay sober to prove them wrong. My grandma pretty much stayed out of my program, unless I asked her to get involved. She did tell my parents that they should let me go to AA as much as I wanted, even if I was being difficult. I have known many young people whose parents would punish them by not allowing them to go to AA meetings. The times I have needed AA the most were when I was not behaving well.

After several years of sobriety, I went to an AA meeting in Chicago, away from my home group. As I was sitting in this meeting, I had déjà vu. It suddenly hit me; my grandma had brought me to my first meeting several months before I got sober. I had always thought my first AA meeting was after I left the psych ward.

Had it not been for my grandma coming before me, I do not know if I would have thought to join AA. I believe she saved me years of suffering. My grandma was ninety-two and sober for twenty-seven years when she died. I have not found it necessary to pick up a drink for the last sixteen years. God willing, one day at a time, maybe I will live to be ninety-two and have seventy-six years of sobriety.

My most cherished inheritance from my grandma is a book of things she wrote down at meetings and a birthday book from her home group, The Big Book Broads. I look at these items and know my grandma lives on in all of the lives she touched, including mine.

CATHY P.

SHERIDAN, WYOMING

CHAPTER FOUR

THANK YOU, OLD-TIMERS

*The love and guidance of seasoned AAs helped these
younger members feel welcome*

"I needed the skill of a very practical sponsor to help me see myself in the older members' stories. Grossly immature, I needed the strong guidance of older members to remain sober," writes the author of a letter to Dear Grapevine.

Those who come years before can often be the key to the young person's recovery. It is wonderful to feel like you fit in with people who are your own age, who share your own generation's culture. But the older members can be the solid examples of sobriety, the ones who extend the hand of acceptance and love, the guides who show the newer member the ropes. Young people, especially those under 20, are still a minority in AA, but in earlier periods it was even rarer to find others in that age group. For a teenager who is used to going out drinking as an activity, sobriety can be a huge social crash. "My old friends realized I wasn't going to party anymore, and I became isolated and lonely," writes an author who was a junior in high school when she got sober. "AA in its love and guidance helped me get through my loneliness."

Even those who come in with a chip on their shoulder soon recognize they need the friendship the older AAs are offering. "The older members of AA that I resented so deeply at first have turned out to be my dearest friends, staunchest supporters, and personal confidants," an author writes. "I no longer believe in generation gaps."

Beyond the sponsorship and emotional support, the old-timers pass on to the young member new ways to have fun and enjoy life sober. "The old-timers told me to come to the club on Saturday night and they would have a prom dance just for me. I was so excited. Two and half years later, I realized that the Covina 502 Club had a dance every Saturday night," writes an author. In this chapter, AAs who started young in sobriety talk about how vital the older members of their groups were to their recovery.

LOVED INTO SOBRIETY
NOVEMBER 1997

I came into the Fellowship when I was sixteen and haven't had a drink since. That was in 1986. In that time I've literally grown up in AA. I've experienced many growing pains, but sobriety has given me a wonderful life, and I'm grateful for this gift that so freely has been given to me. I was fortunate enough to get sober in an area that could be tolerant to such a young, immature person. I love my home group as a family.

Before I came into AA, I was living on the street with whoever would take me in and I was drinking as much as I could. My drinking started in the morning and continued throughout the day. I used everyone around me and had many dangerous experiences. I didn't see myself living to the age of eighteen so I had no plans past the immediate present.

An especially bad episode scared me enough that I asked to be sent to treatment. After I was released, my home group saved me. I found the most loving, accepting group of people. They had a sparkle in their eye and they laughed all of the time. I couldn't remember the last time that I had really laughed. The other members may have had their doubts about my sincerity and requirement for membership, but after they heard me talk they changed their minds.

My group back then was mostly men and mostly over the age of thirty. I felt different because of the age difference but these members never told me to leave. They treated me like any other newcomer. I was always waiting for the angle or for someone to hit on me and it never happened. I was genuinely loved into sobriety. I related to the sharing in the meetings even though I hadn't lost a job, a husband, or kids, because we shared the same pain and hole in the gut due to our drinking.

I had to experience the same growing pains as any other adolescent.

Just because I was sober did not make me exempt from mistakes, and I made many. I didn't always do what was suggested because I was a teenager and most teens think they know everything. But my mistakes were valuable and shaped my character and my life. I'm grateful that I was allowed to make those mistakes with very little criticism. The mistakes were a part of my growing up; they needed to be made. People in my group watched me screw up but didn't hold me back and shared with me their mistakes. They taught me the Steps and told me in a loving manner if I seemed to be straying too far. They celebrated my joys with me and cried with me when the choices I made were bad.

Consequently, I grew up. I married, had children, went to college, found a job, then went back for more school. Every step of the way my group was with me as they watched me struggle with life issues.

From my experiences, I would say that sobriety is about living. My group is in no way my whole life but I attend three meetings a week and volunteer my time when needed. I've seen young people hide in the Fellowship and I find this unfortunate. We've been given such a marvelous gift, so young, that we should live our lives with the same principles outside AA as well. We may live a long life, God willing, and society can benefit from our sober abilities. I am an active member of AA, but I don't hide in AA rooms. I am out there experiencing life.

I have heard some members wishing they had gotten sober at my age, but I don't think they realize what this means. I have grown up and been very aware of my mistakes. Some mistakes even sober are embarrassing due to youthful impulsiveness, and I've had to experience them straight and with no excuses. Young people in AA are likely to make more mistakes only because of their age; we should try to help them by sharing our experience, strength, and hope. I'm not complaining but explaining, so that others can better understand what it's like to grow from a child to an adult in sobriety.

T. F.
BOONE, IOWA

CAPS IN THE AIR
SEPTEMBER 2007

When I got sober, I was a junior in high school. I didn't know how to stay sober among my old partying friends. I went to meetings and heard people say, "Get rid of old playmates and play places." I didn't know how I was going to do that. I couldn't change schools.

My old friends realized I wasn't going to party anymore, and I became isolated and lonely. Occasionally, one of my classmates got sober, but it didn't last long. I listened to people talk about what they watched on TV, and I thought, What's wrong with them? Then I realized that I was the one who was different.

I spent my nights at meetings and at the local coffee house afterward. AA and its love and guidance helped me get through my loneliness. As I approached graduation, I was fearful—I thought about all the parties. My home group threw me the biggest party ever. When my name was called at graduation, the noise that my AA friends made was unbelievable. I thank God for the people in the Fellowship; they loved me when it felt like no one else did. By the time I left school, there were at least thirty people who cared about me and wanted to spend time with me. So far, by the grace of my Higher Power, I've never had to drink again.

CHERYL
FLORIDA

IT WAS HARD TO BELIEVE
MAY 1975

I came to Alcoholics Anonymous when I was twenty-eight years old. It was not my worst drunk that sent me, nor was it the one that caused me the most problems with the law, but it was the worst for me mentally. I had made a contact with AA one year before, and I had walked out of that meeting very disgusted with the caliber of people there, as I saw them, and more disgusted with the things they said. These things made me feel guilty, insecure, and uncertain. So, as had become my pattern, I ran away.

One year later, all the things they had talked about in that meeting were my story. The degeneration of a female alcoholic, the guilt over destroying my family and ruining my young childrens' lives, the loss of friends, and the long record of arrests were all mine in the short span of a year.

I came to AA that day in November 1964 because I finally was bankrupt. I had no friends, no family. Even the Reno, Nevada, city jail wouldn't take me anymore. (I had become accustomed to going there for food, lodging, cigarettes, and a warm place to stay.) I was in the same plight as many people who had gone to AA before—except that I was the youngest person in the Reno area at that time who was obviously, completely, helplessly alcoholic. Ten years ago in my area, there were not many young people in AA.

It was hard for me to come to terms with the fact that people so much older than I was could actually understand the frustration of a young person with a drinking problem. They say God protects fools, and I believe today that he protected this one. I rebelled against the average age of the other group members, though many were providing me with food and lodging and attempting to get me to listen to a way of life that I could not believe would really offer any hope for me.

And yet, somehow, I stayed with AA. For many months, I struggled with the contrast between my own life and their sobriety. Alone, I had many hours to think about the possibility that I really wasn't like them. But when I was with them, their stories began to have an impact on me. The past way of life they talked about and the "acting out" behavior that is referred to in the Big Book were mine, in a different time and a different place, but mine nonetheless.

It wasn't easy to learn to let people help me. I had been running things for many years, since the time I was thirteen and ran away from home. I ran the show once again when I ran away from my first marriage and four children. I ran the show the first time I was ever arrested for being drunk in public, when the police officer was attempting to get me to go home and I was insisting that he arrest me. (After I had insisted for twenty minutes in all the obscene language I could summon, he obliged me.)

For many months, I depended just upon the fellowship of the people of AA, especially in my home group. But when they told me I would have no life unless I relinquished my hold on my old self, I wouldn't listen. Finally, it became obvious to me that I would have to work the Steps of AA to have what they had and what I did not have.

Still very young in my thinking, I balked at all the methods that I had heard about. I made it harder on myself than was necessary, but through that exasperating struggle, I finally came to believe that a power greater than myself had to take over. After all those months in the program, it was clear to me that I could never take command in the running and management of my life.

Since that time, ten years ago, I have not found it necessary to take a drink. The older members of AA that I resented so deeply at first have turned out to be my dearest friends, staunchest supporters, and personal confidants. Many times over, they have shared their experience, strength, and hope with me, and I remain eternally grateful. I remember how my values (which were phony) and my pride once kept me from accepting what those kind, wonderful people had to give. I no longer believe in generation gaps. I know today from experience that history and life repeat themselves, and that the problems of today with alcoholics are just the same as they were many years ago. The only real gap is a gap in communication.

The slang terms change, but resentment is the same today as it was in 1935. Stinking thinking is the same. Lack of faith in the Higher Power is the same. Because AA allowed me to learn these things, I am a better person today, and life is more positive, and I once again have the love of my family and the respect of my children. Most important, the past ten years with AA have let me grow to like myself and to be able to live with myself, one day at a time.

P. B.
CARSON CITY, NEVADA

KID STUFF
DEAR GRAPEVINE, APRIL 2005

In 1980, when I got sober in western Montana, there were a handful of people under twenty-one in our meetings. I was nineteen, and I was sure I wasn't that bad, which sometimes was inadvertently reinforced by older members' comments such as "I've spilled more than you drank" or, "It's good that you've stopped so early in your drinking." I needed the skill of a very practical sponsor to help me see myself in the older members' stories, who showed me how the Big Book applied to me. For instance, when the Book said "sweet relationships were dead" (as a result of alcoholism), I learned to see this as meaning not only marriages, but all the pain I had caused my mother, grandparents, siblings, and friends. Grossly immature, I needed the strong guidance of older members to remain sober.

Service was the key. My sponsor said, "God brought you here to work with other young people like yourself." I will never forget his kindness. I'll be twenty-five years sober in nine days, God willing, and, at forty-four, I finally look like an old-timer. I now advise younger members to answer the comment "I've spilled more than you drank" with this response: "Well, I guess I was a more efficient drunk. I actually got the booze in my mouth!"

KELLEY H.
BOULDER, COLORADO

LISTEN TO PEOPLES' FEELINGS
JULY 1980

I came into the AA program when I was eighteen, back in 1965. Young people weren't the largest group around. In fact, there weren't any AAs my age. No one drank the way I did. Trying to identify on the physical level was hopeless. I was even told I didn't belong in AA, because I was too young and hadn't been drinking long enough.

I'm very grateful for people like my sponsor, who told me it wasn't important how, how much, how often, or even how long I drank. What it did to me was important. So I kept coming back. Even to this day, I think I've run across only one other person who drank the way I did.

I found that my "identifying alikeness" dealt with feelings. I could identify with how people felt. I was afraid, insecure, lonely, paranoid, unhappy. My sponsor told me to listen to peoples' feelings. When I finally did, I found that all the people in those meeting rooms were just like me, whether they were seventy years old or seventeen, whether they only drank hard liquor, beer, or wine, or also popped pills, smoked pot, or shot heroin. What was used on the physical level to deal with the mental, emotional, and spiritual levels was only five to ten percent of the problem. The other ninety to ninety-five percent was living—which I never knew how to do. And that's what I was here in AA for—to learn how to live. I already knew how to die!

So I kept coming back, and I am so grateful that I did. I have a way to live that fills every hole my gut ever had. I need not feel alone or afraid or insecure anymore. I have a Higher Power, which I call God, that fills my every need. I have happiness and joy and peace of mind that walk with me every day. Even when seeming disasters hit, I am able to walk through them. I can have peace in my pain today. These are the gifts and direct results of the Twelve Steps put into living practice.

I spent years looking for things to alienate me, make me different, make me special or unique, better or worse than others (depending on my state of mind). It's easy to dwell on the negative—that was a way of life for me. I was taught through the Steps to start dwelling on the positive—the "alikeness" instead of the differences.

I had to check myself out. Was I still looking for things to alienate me from my fellowman? Was I dwelling on my addiction and seeing how different it was from others', or was I dwelling on my recovery?

You know, God is very wise; being able to see a 360-degree view of life, he sets things into action for the good of the whole. Even if our ant's-eye view can't see the whole picture at one time, it's still there. I truly believe he knew he had a winner with these Twelve Steps; they were put together and written the way they were for the good of the whole.

I am an alcoholic and a drug addict. I may not have drunk exactly the same way as those around me, but the reasons behind it were and are the same. I need to remember this. I need to stay aware— not of the things that alienate me from others, but of the things that bring us together. I am in that lifeboat with everyone else. It's not important what caused the ship to sink. It is important that we all work together to stay afloat!

C. H.
GRANTS, NEW MEXICO

THE GREAT REALITY WITHIN
JANUARY 1995

My name is Anna and I'm an alcoholic. I started drinking at fourteen and by the grace of God I sobered up ten years later. I never drank like a social drinker. The first time I drank I continued until I blacked out. Right away, I drank to get drunk. I woke up sick, throwing up, and not remembering much about the night before. Yet I was excited and looking forward to the next time I could get drunk again.

Before I knew it, I was off and running. I wanted what I wanted when I wanted it and absolutely nothing was going to get in my way. I felt like a powerful truck. I went to any lengths to get drunk and stay drunk. I felt normal only when I was under the influence and totally inadequate when I was sober. Before I knew it, I had a twenty-four-hour-a-day obsession combined with a powerful compulsion to get loaded and stay loaded. If I wasn't intoxicated I was sick and scheming. Just as a car needed gas, I needed alcohol to function. I turned my will and my life over to the care of alcohol.

Insane behavior took over my life. I lied. I stole. I cheated. I associated only with other practicing alcoholics. I was divorced more than once before I was twenty-four years old. Getting beat up wasn't unusual. Courtrooms became a part of my lifestyle. I found myself on federal probation, with mug shots and fingerprints. I received deferred and suspended sentences. I was in and out of mental wards, treatment centers, and halfway houses—at least twelve that I can recall. Detoxing from alcohol became common for me. I felt hopeless.

Meanwhile, I was in and out of AA for over two years. I just wasn't willing to go to any lengths and I wouldn't get honest with myself. Also the God of my understanding was this big man in a robe, with a long white beard, sitting in a big gold chair in heaven, looking down at me.

He had a book with my assets and liabilities. I was doomed. In my mind there was nothing I could do to make the God of my understanding love and forgive me. I was scared of God. I couldn't stay sober with my old concept of God.

The last time I came into AA, on September 6, 1982, an old-timer with seventeen years of sobriety told me to get rid of my concept of God and become as teachable and open-minded as a child who knew nothing. So I did. Every morning I prayed, "God, I don't understand you, but please keep me sober today," and every night I prayed, "God, which I don't understand, thank you for keeping me sober today." I read my devotions every morning and I prayed immediately afterward. I listened to people with sobriety talk about the God of their understanding, and I began to realize that the old God of my understanding was very different from theirs.

I made at least one meeting every day to put at least one hour of sober thinking into my mind. I got a sponsor. I called her all the time. I also got a lot of phone numbers from AA members and I reached out a lot. This was against my nature because I was a loner before I came into AA. But I didn't want to die from alcohol so I did what was suggested. I started reading my Big Book to the best of my ability. My attention span was short and it was difficult for me to concentrate, but I tried and tried. I didn't want to die from alcohol.

Changes took place. I had new friends. I wasn't physically sick anymore. I came to believe that a power greater than myself could restore me to sanity. I took one Step at a time with the guidance of my sponsor. One day I read the most beautiful lines in the Big Book. These lines helped me form a God of my understanding, and I haven't found it necessary to drink in over five years.

"We found the Great Reality deep down within us. In the last analysis it is only there that He may be found. It was so with us."

ANNA S.
FAIRVIEW, OKLAHOMA

PROM NIGHT
MAY 2007

I was as desperate as only the dying can be when I called our Central Office in Covina, California, and spoke with a woman named Gloria. It was around 5:30 P.M. on December 25, and I'd just come to for the last time. I was seventeen years old and in real bad shape. Gloria told me there was a meeting starting in an hour and asked if I could make it to the meeting without taking a drink, and if, as a courtesy, I would take a shower first. I told her I did not know if I could not drink, but I was willing to try real hard not to drink before the meeting. It was a long three-mile drive to the meeting place, and I was so focused on being on time that I was shocked when I made it without taking a drink. The only thing I remember about the first meeting was that I was there and that I had not had a drink all day. At the end, everyone stood up, held hands, and said, "Keep coming back!" And that's what I did, every day, three to four times a day.

I detoxed in the meetings with women telling me that the floor was not moving, spiders were not crawling on me, and "this too shall pass." I remember how thrilled I was when I was given my first full cup of coffee in a meeting because I had stopped shaking and I was still sober.

The old-timers sat me down in front of the window facing the street so that when my parents drove by they could see me in the meetings. I was told that AA was not a day care for juvenile delinquents. This was about life or death. They also told me that just because we get sober does not mean that our responsibilities end. My job was to get my high school diploma. When I showed up before twelve noon at the clubhouse, the old-timers called my truant officer and had me taken to school. They did this so often that my truant officer began picking me up at the park where I lived, took me to school, picked me up from school, and then took me to the 12:30 P.M. meeting.

On the night I graduated from high school, as I stepped up when my name was called, the old-timers and my truant officer cheered louder than all the rest who cheered for the students who'd gone before me. But I was the only student not invited to attend the prom. I was told that I was not the kind of influence welcomed at the school prom. I was devastated. I had worked so hard, but drinking took me to places that parents feared. Alcohol was not a topic discussed at the time; it was still a dirty little secret.

Those old-timers really felt bad for me. They knew of my pain from their own experiences. So they told me to come to the club on Saturday night and they would have a prom dance just for me. I was so excited. They really did care about me! I danced every dance. I was brought sodas, my cigarettes were lit, and doors were opened for me. The night was mine, all mine. This dance was done just for me! I was special! It was the best night ever, and I was clean and sober.

Two and half years later, I was drinking coffee at the clubhouse at about 10:00 P.M. on a Saturday night when I realized that the Covina 502 Club had a dance every Saturday night. My prom dance was not about me at all. It was what the old-timers did every Saturday night. I began to laugh at how self-centered I was to think that it was all about me and how dumb I was that it took me two and half years to figure it out.

What I learned is that my sobriety was important to the old-timers of the day. The men and women who were sober when I entered the rooms of Alcoholics Anonymous in 1979 cared that I not just get sober, but that I stay clean and sober one day at a time. I mattered in God's world. Looking back all these years later (twenty-eight years now!), I see that my first ninety days were like having a baby: You forget the pain and celebrate the miracle for the rest of your life—one day at a time.

CAROL O.
PENSACOLA, FLORIDA

CHAPTER FIVE

THERE WERE OTHERS JUST LIKE ME

Connecting with their own age group and having fun sober
was the beginning of the end of isolation

In the first story in this chapter, a very young AA relies mostly on older members for the first five years of her sobriety. She then slowly morphs into YPAA groups as she feels more comfortable. "At 24 and sober for nine-and-a-half years, my home group is a young peoples' meeting. I'm no longer the youngest member there, and I can enjoy being looked to as an elder stateswoman."

These stories talk about feeling different, angry, isolated, unwanted, unprepared and terrorized about the notion of life without alcohol. "Being young, we recover fast physically, and some old-timers believe we're doing great. But our insides still boil like mad," writes one author. "I had to have someone to relate to and get help from."

Young AAs frequently write about having to learn how to live. One author writes that home group members "had to teach me, by example, how to enjoy life and have fun sober. I began to realize there would be fewer amends to make if I had fun without hurting others. I learned how to take responsibility for my actions."

And then there are the YPAA conferences, including the big one— ICYPAA, the International Conference of Young People in AA—which draws thousands. Yes, this conference is about service, the Twelve Steps and Traditions, and other recovery tools and topics. But for many young people, it is the first time it hits them—they really can have fun without a drink. A member describes a first YPAA experience:

"I was overwhelmed with excitement. The energy in the room is incredible. I have never been to any other AA event where so many sober alcoholics are in one room, having the time of their lives."

No longer feeling alone is the overriding theme of the stories that follow.

THE YOUNG ONE
JULY 2009

Since my first meeting, I have felt the sense of camaraderie that the Big Book describes. I was blessed to walk into a welcoming group. My parents walked me up to the church and kind folks on the entrance steps told them, "We'll take her from here. The meeting ends at 9. You can pick her up shortly after that." A man named Charlie handed me my first Big Book and guided me into the beginner's meeting. At my second meeting, Sarah extended her hand and pronounced herself my sponsor. I felt welcome.

I walked into these halls at 14, which means my first three years as a member of Alcoholics Anonymous were without a driver's license. I joined an older group—its core membership being a group of men and women 20 or 30 years my senior with long-term sobriety. The women of my home group joked about being soccer moms, calling one another to figure out, "Who's got Danna?" My parents usually dropped me off for the meeting; the AAs handled the rest. I was always brought along to dinner or the movies. My age mattered less than the fact that I identified as an alcoholic. I had a ride home even when it was out of the way or late at night. The women from my home group threw me a surprise high school graduation party and pooled to buy me a wonderful gift.

From my first meeting until now, I remain in awe of the genuineness and unconditional love of AA members.

My membership in that older group lasted about four or five years. My sponsor was the same age as my mother (and they got to be close friends!). Although some young people cycled through the group, I was the only one who remained a sober member. I attended the one young peoples' meeting in the area for my first 90 days of sobriety. I stopped shortly after, realizing I only went to smoke cigarettes and flirt with boys. In retrospect, I think I was too young for it. Many of my group's members had long-term sobriety, and I craved the stability they offered. The clamors of my uncomfortable adolescence could be checked at the door when I entered that church basement.

In the five years since I've left my hometown and that home group, I have gradually become more immersed in YPAA (our affectionate acronym for Young People in AA.) It has been a quiet and slow transition for me. I attribute this to the fact that, at 18 or 19 years old, I was often still the youngest member in many meetings. Now, at 24 and sober for nine-and-a-half years, my home group is a young peoples' meeting. I'm no longer the youngest member there, and I can enjoy being looked to as an "elder stateswoman." I am out socializing four or five nights a week with a group of AAs my age: eating dinner, attending concerts and having fun.

Young peoples' AA felt too much like high school, with its incessant gossip and late nights.

At most YPAA meetings and conferences, I hear members share stories of not feeling comfortable in AA until attending a YP meeting. They admit to feeling excluded or different in "big peoples' AA." I am fortunate to have never heard put-downs such as "I spilled more than you drank." I was able to identify and not compare for my first few years of meetings. I never worried that I hadn't lost a husband or family—getting kicked out of high school and crashing a car were enough for me. Within YPAA, many believe they could never have gotten sober without other young people. This may be true for some, but it is not so for me. I still crave the stability of different types of meetings.

Big peoples' AA saved my life. Now, I'm in a place where I can repay some of that debt and help others. I feel a responsibility to share that it's possible for a young person to get sober anywhere, in any group.

DANNA F.
WALTHAM, MASSACHUSETTS

SOBRIETY COUNTDOWN
JUNE 1983

It was mid-August 1982, in New York City, when 1,200 sober alcoholics gathered for the Twenty-Fifth International Conference of Young People in AA (ICYPAA). One of the highlights of the weekend of sharing was Saturday night's sobriety countdown. There we were in the enormous ballroom, representing numerous states and several countries, and we were asked to stand when our year or month or week (!) of sobriety was called.

At forty-seven years (then the age of our dear Fellowship), there were none who could stand. Remember, we were mostly of the under-forty generation. At twenty-seven, one did stand, and he received enthusiastic applause. As the count went down to the single-digit years, many more stood up. I was one of the group with three years of sobriety, and it seemed that there were over a hundred of us. I loved it!

But the best part was yet to come. After the call for one year of sobriety, the count was by months: eleven, ten (a sizable number stood). Then, it was three weeks, two weeks, one week of sobriety—the shivers were getting us all. Six days, five days, and ultimately the most important and memorable for all of us in AA: one day of sobriety! The place went nuts when one lone young man named Michael stood up. We all started cheering so loudly, I thought the hotel people must be wondering whether we hadn't all decided to break out at once. Michael was the most important person in that room of 1,200 sober alcoholics—and we let him know it.

The chairperson of the entire ICYPAA weekend practically leaped over tables with the Big Book clutched to his chest. As a couple of Michael's new friends raised him to their shoulders, the chairperson gave him the Big Book, hugged him warmly, and wished him one more day of sobriety. That's what it's all about—one moment of caring for one other alcoholic. I am glad and grateful to be a part of AA. Today, I know the joy of living.

H. P.
BOSTON, MASSACHUSETTS

YOUNG PEOPLES' GROUPS
JULY 1969

My first contact with AA was in Buffalo, N.Y., over eleven years ago, at the age of twenty-three. The number of young people in AA was small, and I was lost and lonely as ever. I could identify readily with the members' stories, as I'd been in bad shape from day one, but how to get well was something else. I stayed sober purely on guts for almost two years.

This is probably the most significant problem the young person faces: He has little or no productive past, and organizing a life terrifies him. Being young, we recover fast physically, and some old-timers believe we're doing great. But our insides still boil like mad. It appears that members of young peoples' groups have faced this fact and begun to challenge each other's fronts. We pretend not to care about a job, a wife, a car, or anything else that is brought up, until somebody finally sits us down and tells us about fear of failure.

In Buffalo, and later in Colorado Springs, it seemed to me that AA people thought it was great for young people to join, but when it came to really "allowing" us to participate in group activities, that never happened. Feeling left out of society and merely tolerated really bugs many of us. I will add here that these sick feelings I had didn't help the group to warm to me, but many of us come to AA in that kind of shape.

In 1961, in Denver, I finally sobered up again and walked into a group with a new attitude: I am here, and I will get in, and I will get well in spite of my sick feelings, fears, hates. After a while, I realized that other young people weren't staying. I had to have someone to relate to and get help from. So some of us got together to form a young peoples' group.

It had been tried before, and had failed. Over and over we heard that it was unnecessary and that ours would fold as the other had. Being an unpopular group, we were not particular about who came in, and we had all kinds. We struggled, and were still there to welcome the International Conference of Young People, held July 1967, in Denver. Yet the only thing we ever did in that early group was talk about us and how we really felt before and after getting sober. Had I not been forced to be responsible for my group, show up every week, and talk about me, I doubt if I'd be here and sober today.

In these groups, it's pretty hard to put up a front when everyone around you has the same hang-ups. That is the second significant characteristic of young peoples' groups. When you take the bottle away from a young, active, hostile, antisocial character, you have the same character, minus bottle. It is probably hard for any group to stomach this opinionated, obnoxious cat. Therefore, he doesn't fit in well and ends up with little activity in the group and few friends. In a young peoples' group, most of us were or are like this, and the group can understand and survive such behavior until the newcomer settles into the group. Like any group, most of us have lots of problems, but the understanding among us and the talking about ourselves prevail. I'm sure these facts are true of other groups too, but I think they are most important in young peoples' groups.

Surprisingly, the problem of sex is not any bigger than in other groups. Some chasing goes on, as it does in any group of people. Most groups and individuals I've met face the problem with a good degree of honesty. Drug addiction is a problem in many groups, but here we have a slight advantage. A young addict who comes to one of our groups is accepted provided he remembers it is an AA group. Between the alcoholics and the addicts, the problem is usually faced; help is offered; and the person either gets well or gets lost, without spreading his problem to the sick alcoholic who is trying to get well. The pill-head poses a real problem. Most young people who have been around awhile seem pretty adamantly antimedication. They feel most of us can survive without it and should suffer a little so that we will stick close to the group.

According to the World Directory and local financial statements, the financial contributions of young peoples' groups to GSO and Central Offices or Intergroups appear to be very low. Most of our groups are very poor. Many young people do not recover financially for a long time. Divorce, becoming more prevalent yearly, is one big cause. Many young men I know are either hung with high support payments or are running from them and are afraid to get good jobs. Many others have little or no employment background, and therefore end up starting out at low-salaried jobs.

Many view a young peoples' group as an immature bunch. That is probably true; often, the members include few stable, longtime-sober people. Good members with one, two, or three years of sobriety sometimes seem to gravitate to more mature groups as they grow, and then they only occasionally show up at young peoples' meetings. Although this keeps the group small and immature, it also keeps it from getting too big and creating a schism.

Also, we do not wish to draw our members away from the general run of AA activities in their areas. We want to participate in AA—all of it; but some of us do better if we first share our inexperience among ourselves.

J. G.
SAN FRANCISCO, CALIFORNIA

BACK-UP PLAN SCRAPPED
DEAR GRAPEVINE, AUGUST 2010

I am 20 years old and have been battling alcoholism since I was 12. I couldn't stay sober for more than six hours. I was dying and alone, and couldn't imagine life getting better, but I decided to try treatment one last time, with suicide as my back-up plan.

Rehab introduced me to the longest period of sobriety I'd known, and to AA. In one of the meetings I found a flyer from the International Conference of Young People in Alcoholics Anonymous (ICYPAA). The Tuesday following my release from rehab I went to a meeting organizing a bus trip to Atlanta, Ga., for ICYPAA. I had no money but someone decided to drag me along. We left the next day.

Can you imagine 3,000 young people in AA together celebrating sobriety and life? It was mind-blowing. They were excited about recovery and their enthusiasm was contagious. It rubbed off on me and for the first time in a long time thoughts of suicide and drinking left my mind; I wanted to live and to find the happiness I felt there. What's even cooler than that is I realized that I wasn't alone. There are others just like me all over the world recovering with the Twelve Steps of AA. Georgia gave me more hope than I could have ever dreamed of. Now—10 months later and almost nine months sober—I sit here writing this story as one of the many young people in AA.

TANYA A.
MUKWONAGO, WISCONSIN

GROW OR GO
OCTOBER 1997

was 17 years old and knew deep down I was different from my fel-
lows. Having never tried because of fear, I believed I couldn't not
drink even though I said I could. I "volunteered" for a treatment
center after some loving encouragement from a high school counsel-
or who said, "Go to treatment or don't come back here." At the center,
I was introduced to my first Alcoholics Anonymous meeting—the
Monday Night Young Peoples' Group.

At that meeting, I was welcomed by what seemed like hundreds of
handshakes. The greeting committee was very active. I was unaware at
the time of a recent group inventory that had addressed the need for
such a committee, but I was very aware of how welcome I felt. There
were almost one hundred people in the main discussion meeting. Beginners classes were held every Monday night, and we were strongly
encouraged to attend all of them before joining the main meeting.
Taking this suggestion gave me a solid foundation of sponsorship, the
Twelve Steps, and a Higher Power. It was a very powerful gathering of
young AAs. Some of them felt unaccepted at other meetings in town.
This group, I believe, gained much of its energy from the fact that we
needed each other so much.

As young people, our behavior sometimes was not that "recovered"
when it came to "all of our affairs." I sometimes learned the hard way.
Members of the group had to teach me, by example, how to enjoy life
and have fun sober. I began to realize there would be fewer amends to
make if I had fun without hurting others. I learned how to take responsibility for my actions.

I learned about the group and the Twelve Traditions from AA
members who put the common welfare of the group above their
own. We did group inventories annually to see how to better reach

suffering alcoholics. We tried everything possible to carry the message, from day care to deaf interpreters. I didn't want to go to these "boring" inventories at first; I preferred one of the beginners classes instead. My sponsor pointed out that the inventory was an AA meeting and that every part of this spiritual program belonged in a group discussion. He said that all the issues we would discuss were about being responsible and carrying the AA message. He told me that God worked through an informed group conscience and that every home group member was part of a larger whole and might contribute to that. My group did its best to let the hand of AA be there for the still-suffering alcoholic. I learned how to be a sober member of Alcoholics Anonymous.

After five years of sobriety, literally growing up in that group, it was time to learn another valuable lesson: letting go. I had bounced from job to job for a while, tried college, and begun a family. I decided to join the army. I cried when I said goodbye to the group. They told me it was time to go, that God had a plan and would take care of me wherever my journey led me. I left knowing I would be okay. I also knew enough to find the Fellowship as soon as I got somewhere new. I did just that seven years ago, and I've stayed sober ever since.

Recently, I visited my hometown and found that my old home group is now much smaller and has moved to a new location. The people I got sober with have grown up and moved on just as I did. Young people are sober in nearly every group in that large city. I used to be the youngest one in most meetings by about ten years; now there are teenagers sober in the suburb where I grew up. Change is a part of life, especially in AA where we must grow or go. That group is exactly what God wants it to be today, but I thank him with all of my heart that it was exactly the way it was when I walked through the doors of my very first AA meeting.

I participate in Alcoholics Anonymous today and try to be an example to all. Today I have a new home group in a new town and I try to bring the spirit of that first one to my new one and make it the best in the world. If you don't believe that your home group is the best in the world, don't find a new one: stay where you are and put your whole heart into it. God put you there for a reason.

ROGER W.
HONOLULU, HAWAII

LIFE, UNLIMITED
SEPTEMBER 2007

For most teenagers, navigating the social and emotional nightmare of high school is hard enough, but doing it as a newcomer to sobriety seemed impossible. My solution to high school while I was drinking was simple: Don't go. So I didn't.

School seemed stupid. There was always something way more interesting to do. After a while, I couldn't sit in a class even when I wanted to. The school and my mom kept trying to get me to show up, but I just couldn't stay. I would be at school and that itch would come. I needed to get out of there. I would tell myself that I would come back for my next class, but I was always too loaded to go back. It was easier to just drop out. Of course, no one else (including my mom) was on board with my decision, so I had to run away from home to continue the lifestyle I wanted. I spent the next year or so running wild. I finally hit bottom and sobered up (with a little help from the juvenile justice system) two weeks after my sixteenth birthday.

Readjusting to teenage life was a struggle. I had been independent and doing very dangerous things with very dangerous people. I hadn't had a friend my own age in a long time. I didn't feel like I should have to follow the same rules as other teenagers. I had been leading what I considered an adult life, so I should be treated like an adult, right? It was a miracle that I was sober and that I came home at night. As far as I was concerned, my mom should recognize that and lay off. She didn't agree.

A lot of compromise had to happen. I had to learn that my mom didn't owe me anything. In fact, as I learned through my inventory, I owed her daily amends for the vast amount of pain and suffering I put her though.

Getting me back into school was a top priority for her and the courts. I don't know how well I would have handled a huge school with 3,000 kids, especially with the reputation I had. I was too far behind to go back to a regular school, but this turned out to be a blessing in disguise.

I was referred to continuation school, the so-called "bad kid" school. I didn't know how I could stay sober around all those kids. I had no idea that I was about to walk into a place that would become one of the pillars of my early sobriety. When I met with the principal to enroll, I was totally taken aback by how up front he was with me. He introduced himself simply as "Doc." The first question he asked me was whether or not I wanted to stay sober. Then he let me know that if I chose not to, school was not going to work for me and he was not going to put up with it. I was shocked. No one in a school had ever been so blunt with me.

Then he told me that there was a sobriety support group once a week and I was welcome to participate. I said I would think about it. There were several students at this school who I was friends with from meetings, and they convinced me that I should participate.

Sobriety group was great. Not everybody in group went to meetings, but the majority did, and it was a great place to find out which meetings had young people in them.

I quickly learned that all of the teachers and staff were 100 percent supportive of my sobriety. I had never experienced that kind of openness and honesty with "authority figures." I felt like they were on my side, not like they were out to get me. I got to experience the ups and downs of early sobriety in a totally safe school environment. They were so understanding of what I was going through. Many days, the very best I was capable of was to just stay put and not get loaded. I felt like I was coming out of my skin, so the thought of doing schoolwork seemed ridiculous. Doc let me cry in his office with my sober friends when I needed to. He also let us leave early to go to the noon meeting at a local clubhouse. My English teacher baked me cookies every time I took a token. One of my teachers broke his anonymity to me and told me he had been sober thirteen years in AA. I was given the room I needed to figure out how to function.

It helped so much to have other sober young people to talk to. It kept me from feeling like a freak when I went back to high school. I felt out of place in the world already, so I felt really out of place around other teenagers. They seemed trite and caught up in unimportant social drama and childish problems. I had real problems. The only place I felt like I fit was at meetings. I learned from other AAs that these feelings were not about the other kids, but that it was my alcoholic ego that made me feel different from everybody else.

Being an alcoholic and a teenager is a double whammy in terms of impulsiveness and self-centeredness. In a less understanding environment, my behavior may have been taken as "defiant" or "maladjusted," and I may have been kicked out or dropped out. I'll be the first to admit that I was defiant and maladjusted, but the staff had insight and a knowledge of alcoholism. They understood that I would get better if I stayed sober, and I needed someone to stick it out with me. I had to learn to apply the Steps in my life, and that meant at school and with other kids—kids who didn't have to do things like make amends and practice restraint of pen and tongue. I had to do these things no matter how they acted. One of the hardest amends I had to make was to one of my teachers for cheating in her class (in sobriety). But my sponsor and other AAs walked me through it.

By the start of my senior year, I was totally caught up. At my school I had earned status as a leader, and my teachers started nominating me for scholarships and awards! It was a totally new experience. Of course, my alcoholic insecurities were still alive and well—now I was self-conscious about being a "teachers pet" instead of a troublemaker. But once again, having AA and sober friends on and off campus helped me to walk through my fear and insecurity. I was given the opportunity to share my experience with teenagers by speaking in health classes and assemblies at other schools. I loved doing it.

I got my first Twelfth Step call when a school counselor at one of the local junior high schools called my school counselor. She knew there were "sober kids" at my school. She had a thirteen-year-old girl who thought she needed help. My counselor asked me if I would go and talk to her. I went right over to her school and met her in the office. The counselor left us alone and I proceeded to tell the girl my AA story, just as the Big Book instructs. I gave her my phone number and told her that I would take her to a meeting if she wanted. That girl is still sober today.

High school was such a powerful experience for me that I got a job there after I graduated. I have come full circle. I am a supportive staff member and a good example of AA to students who are in recovery, as well as to students who may one day need it. I break my anonymity with students (as was done for me) when I feel that I can be of service.

All of my coworkers saw me as a shaky sixteen-year-old newcomer, so they send students who may benefit from my experience to talk with me all the time. I now facilitate the support group that meant so much to me as a student. I have a couch in my office and students hang out when they need to talk or just simply sit until they feel better.

My high school experience not only helped me form a strong foundation for my sobriety, it helped me develop an academic foundation as well. Likewise, my foundation in Alcoholics Anonymous gave me the tools and support I needed to stay in school when the going got tough. Sometimes those cheesy AA sayings—"Keep putting one foot in front of the other" and "Suit up and show up"—were the only things that kept me from dropping out.

I have since graduated with honors from college and I am looking forward to starting graduate school. Once, I thought sobriety meant that I would have to live with limited options in my life. My experience has been exactly the opposite. I spent a semester studying in another country, sober. I had the time of my life and experienced international AA at twenty years of age. I have not found it necessary to take a drink through five years of college, my twenty-first birthday, or most recently, my wedding. Having dedicated educators in my early sobriety helped me to realize that I want to always remain "teach-able," not only academically, but in life.

DIANA C.
OCEANSIDE, CALIFORNIA

IT WAS ALL NEW TO ME
FEBRUARY 2010

Being a teenage alcoholic often places a person into an interesting set of circumstances when he sobers up. I joined AA when I was 18 in the Midwest. There were very few young people and no or-ganized young peoples' groups, committees or conferences for me to attend. For me, identification happened slowly and opportunities to get involved in committee-level service came even more slowly. Even becoming a sponsor took a while. People who asked me were often 10-15 years older than me and were either not serious about recovery from alcoholism or had life problems I had never experienced. For an alcoholic whose life depends on Twelfth Step work, times were sometimes rough.

None of this was new to me since I was just coming out of foster care and had been largely unsuccessful in any kind of social environ-ment. I had often felt alienated and alone as a combined result of my alcoholism and my life's path. On one hand, AA gave me a place to be. On another, it sometimes lacked the accountability that a person gains from true peers. Old-timers were just happy I was coming to AA and staying sober. They shared their experience with me, which was usual-ly related to how their kids were like me. It wasn't until I found Young Peoples' AA (YPAA), that people started to say things like, "I am about to finish my last college class and I am still sober!" When I started to hear those kinds of things, it started me on a path from an 8th grade education all the way to a master's degree. I am 31 years old now and have 13 years of sobriety, made possible by AA's Twelve Steps, Twelve

Traditions, sponsorship and heaps of service work.

I got involved in YPAA after I moved to San Diego, Calif. There people kept talking about a committee for young people called the Greater San Diego Young People in AA (GSDYPAA). I lived pretty far from where they met and later became involved with a more local committee that formed called the North San Diego Young People in AA (NSDYPAA). All of a sudden, I had great amounts of responsibility. Initially, I took the commitment of program chair, which meant that whenever we hosted a dance, dodge ball tournament or campout, I set up the meetings that were attached to the event. Later I became a treasurer, and I kept track of an account and a ledger—all new to me! Finally I became our bid package chairman. We were bidding to host the state young peoples' conference.

Assembling a bid package was an arduous process. We had to negotiate contracts with potential hotels, present up-to-date treasury records, and demonstrate participation in our area assemblies, area committees and intergroup. We organized a skit to show our unity as a committee at the state conference. We got to dance, act, recite poetry or sing, relaying the AA message in dramatic fashion. What a rush, and what a great fit for a young person in AA! Most of us were in tears by the end. We didn't even expect to be picked to host the All California Young People in AA (ACYPAA) Round Up; we just knew what we had all been through together. One person had had a suicide attempt; another's father was in the hospital after an alcohol-related incident; some had graduated from universities; I myself had gotten married. We had fought in business meetings, and now we cried together. It was a beautiful experience for all of us.

Leading up to the conference, we had been active in service all year. We had thrown dances and other fun events and we had co-hosted events with local districts and area committees. We spoke on hospitals and institutions (H&I) panels, and participated in Bridging the Gap commitments. I was working full-time and finishing graduate school during all of this. What a ride!

At the Saturday night main meeting at the ACYPAA conference, the

ACYPAA advisory council was going to announce which of the 11 California bid cities had been awarded the conference for 2010. The council was made up of young people who had all hosted the conference in the past; they were seen as a leadership body to a lot of us. Amid an enthusiastic crowd of 2,700 people screaming, "Where are we going?" our committee waited, holding hands and standing up on our chairs.

Then a member of the council walked up to the microphone with his cell phone, which had the song from our bid skit playing over the loud speakers! Our whole committee started jumping up and down, hugging and crying.

Being chosen to be custodians of AA's message for the young people of California for this year's ACYPAA both humbled us and overwhelmed us. God's touch was palpable.

We spent all year planning the conference. We are still fighting and crying and hugging, as happens in AA committees working toward a common goal with varied experiences. We looked for the best ways we could serve, and traveled all over doing outreach for the conference. California is a big state and there were a lot of young people to get the word out to.

I have to say, though, nothing satisfies me more than when I visit a meeting in a small desert town that knows nothing about ACYPAA. I get to share this message with a newcomer—who looks and talks an awful lot like I did in my early Midwest meetings, when I was out of touch and had no idea what God had in store for me down the road.

KANSAS C.
OCEANSIDE, CALIFORNIA

SAY NO TO NOTHING
FEBRUARY 2010

As I entered the hotel lobby, I looked up at the massive 60 floors and thought, Wow, I wonder if I'll ever run into a drunk who could tell me where I can find a meeting. I set down my bags, went out for a smoke, and was kidnapped by ICYPAA old-timers. I got back about 13 hours later with two other AAs who crashed in my bed. After two hours of sleep, I jumped out of bed and yearned for more. That was two days before the conference actually started. I was completely unaware that even with jet-lag, I would total six hours of sleep in five days, and that a day later the hotel would be shut down by ICYPAA's massive crowd. There were countless people walking up to the hotel to look inside and say, "What's going on in there, can we come in?"

I have truly been rocketed into a fourth dimension I never knew existed. I always believed I would experience the Promises in my life, but I never expected them to all be thrown at me over one short weekend. I stood in the meeting room with 3,500 drunks under the age of 30, and I had chills running down my spine and tears in my eyes. Little did I know this was the mere beginning—the pre-conference speaker. I stood on my chair and danced to Bob Marley. After all, this was why I came; however, I was feeling very uncomfortable and uncool.

Then, in a brief moment of silence, I realized we were doubled in size because with each one of us young people stood our Higher Power. The spirituality in the room could have knocked me over. I took a second to recompose myself, then I leaned over to my new friend, with his green, red and yellow mohawk, and said, "This is it." He smiled and looked down at me and just said, "Yeah, ha-ha, awesome, right?" I knew at that moment I had found that feeling I had chased since my first drink: total acceptance, absolute love and a freedom to act stupid.

The first bit of advice I received was very useful. I was riding through

Atlanta in the back of a pickup truck, and the "old-timers," who had been to at least three ICYPAAs before, said, "Say no to nothing, do it all, and sleep as little as possible." My instant thought was, Yeah right. I am a recluse now that I am sober. I am not the party girl I once was. There is no way in hell I could stay up late or let my hair down in front of all these people.

But before I knew it, I was on the stage at a nightclub full of sober people, raving with the D.J. I stopped and thought, Can this be right? Can this be spiritual? Can sobriety be so much fun? I asked God for an intuitive thought or decision, only to be thrown back into reality by a song that said, "Shut up and dance." At that moment I was released from the bondage of self. I knew, at that moment, I had found my place in this world.

I made friends from all over the U.S., Canada, Jamaica, England and Tokyo. They nicknamed me "Germany" and I quite liked it. Hell, it beat my old nicknames of "shakie," "pukie" or "nakie."

At the beginning of each meeting, the speaker would introduce him or herself, "Hi, I am _____ and I am an alcoholic," and then the thousands of young people would return with, "Hi, _____ , we love you, _____ , lots and lots and lots and WHOOOOOLE BUNCHES! Whooo!" (This was accompanied by a group pelvic thrust toward the speaker which seemed to get bigger later in the weekend). And in "How it Works," when the line, "What an order! I can't go through with it," was read, everyone would yell, "B _____ t!"

That is the attitude I left with. If you think you can't enjoy life in sobriety, "B _____ t!" There was so much power, gratitude and inspiration in Atlanta that I can never imagine having the desire to drink return to me, and, God willing, it will not. But if it does, I am so grateful to have AA, young or old, to turn to.

We are the next generation of old-timers, the future of this Fellowship. We, young people in AA around the world, are on fire with recovery.

CARLY B.
STUTTGART, GERMANY

CHAPTER SIX

THE TURNING POINT

That moment they realized that they really can't drink safely

"It's unfortunate that it took an accident and the death of my friend to turn my life around, but that's what happened," writes the author of "A Homegrown Drunk." "The seed had been planted." More than one young AA in this chapter uses that phrase to describe his or her moment of truth—the turning point.

This is the moment when a young person lets go of any doubt that he or she is an alcoholic, or that he or she can drink safely, or that he or she doesn't belong in this meeting—this Fellowship. Sometimes these moments occur during the last run, sometimes several years before coming to AA, or sometimes even in sobriety.

"I said, 'God, I'm going to drink unless there's someone in this coffee shop I can talk to about this stuff,'" a member writes. And there are two AAs at the counter, more than willing to listen.

Moments like that can seem profound. Another author talks about wanting to drink, even after surviving a horrific drinking-related motorcycle crash not long before. He shares this at a meeting, and the man who had saved his life during that crash happens to be there. The young AA considers it is a miracle. "A chill ran up my spine. I still had the bloodstained T-shirt, and now, in an AA meeting, I was to meet the man who had placed it under my head."

Not everyone has a momentous awakening. Sometimes it's the words of a therapist hitting a nerve, sometimes it's an ex, an old drinking partner suddenly looking confident and clear-eyed.

"I said, 'Where the hell have you been?' She said, 'In detox for 30 days. AA meetings every day after that.' My old girlfriend made my drinking even worse because now I knew there was a way out."

The party was over. In the next pages, these and other members tell how the seed of AA was planted in their lives.

CLOSE ENCOUNTERS OF THE COFFEE SHOP KIND
JANUARY 1998

By the grace of a very loving God, I've been a sober member of Alcoholics Anonymous since January 18, 1988. I say "by the grace of God" because I'm one of those people who truly believe I've lost the power of choice when it comes to drink. I could not will myself into sobriety (believe me, I tried) nor can I maintain my sobriety on my own willpower (I attempted that as well). I do believe I have one choice when it comes to my sobriety and it certainly isn't the choice of whether to drink or not. My choice is this: I can improve my relationship with my Higher Power by working the Twelve Steps daily (for all I have is a daily reprieve) or being alcoholic, I can drink. The interesting part is that if I'm improving my relationship with my Higher Power on a daily basis I can't drink, no matter how badly I may want to. So if I want to stay sober I must focus on improving my conscious contact with God.

The Big Book of Alcoholics Anonymous states: "The alcoholic at certain times has no effective mental defense against the first drink." I have personally experienced this lack of power at least once in the past nine years. It was my twenty-fourth birthday and I had just over five years sober. I was a student at UCLA (another gift of sobriety) and was very close to graduating. My studies were strenuous and my participation in sobriety was at a low point. I remember being resentful because very few people called me on my birthday, though I'd failed to tell anyone that it was coming up. The next thing I knew I was on my way to a classmate's house to celebrate my birthday with a bottle of vodka. On the way there, I stopped at a local coffee shop to make a phone call and had a moment of clarity. I thought that perhaps I should give God one last chance. Rebelliously I said, "God, I'm going to drink unless there's someone in this coffee shop I can talk to about this stuff." I walked into the coffee shop and didn't recognize anyone. I thought, That's it, I'm going to drink. I made my phone call and was walking out of the shop when I recognized two men sitting together having coffee. I'd never talked to either one of them but I'd seen them at meetings. I asked if I could sit with them and I proceeded to tell them about the obsession that had overtaken me. They listened and shared their experience, strength, and hope with me. The miracle didn't stop there. A few minutes later a man sat near us and I started chatting with him. He told me his drinking was out of hand and he wanted to stop. I took him to a meeting the following night, he asked me to be his sponsor, and we took the Steps together.

Every time I think of this experience, I am amazed. I was on my way to getting drunk that night and instead I ended up sponsoring another alcoholic.

This experience forced me to reevaluate the program I'd been working in the previous months. In doing so, I made a great personal realization that I've been sharing in meetings ever since. My realization was this: If I don't consciously take the Twelve Steps forward each day of my life, I will unconsciously take the Twelve Steps backward and that will lead me to drink. It is subtle and I may not even know it's happening, but it indeed happens.

ANONYMOUS
SANTA MONICA, CALIFORNIA

HE GAVE ME THE SHIRT OFF HIS BACK
DECEMBER 1994

My name is Bill and I'm an alcoholic. Before I had my last drink in July 1986, it was necessary for me to try every form of self-deception and experimentation that the Big Book refers to. I found myself in and out of Alcoholics Anonymous for about eight years. I became familiar with the program and could recite large portions of the

Big Book from memory. Even so, I kept right on drinking. My unsuccessful attempts at the AA way of life led me to believe I was doomed to a miserable future of drinking that surely would end in tragedy.

I openly balked when the Promises were read, and thought that I'd have to be a simpleton like the others for the Steps to work for me. Then one night, much to my surprise, I was in a meeting with my hand raised. It had been a very difficult day for me and I was overcome with a feeling of guilt for a decision I had recently made.

To the group I expressed my desire to ride my newly purchased motorcycle at full speed on the highway and lay it down. I went on to give the reasons for my wish to die. Following a nearly fatal accident I had been in only six months earlier, I promised my dear mother I'd never ride again. It was she who had nursed me back to health, and I felt that the least I could do to repay her was keep my promise. Now, I had just gone out and bought a new motorcycle. Coupled with the unbearable guilt this had brought on was the pitiful and incomprehensible demoralization that my attempts at controlled drinking had led to. So, now my dilemma was twofold: I was unable to imagine life with or without alcohol, and I was unable to imagine life with or without a motorcycle. Truly, I was at the jumping-off place and wished for the end.

After I had finished talking, a man named Lee shared. He said he could identify with me because he'd seen an accident similar to the one I had described. He went on to tell of the night he was at an AA meeting and heard a nightmarish collision on the highway just outside. He left the meeting so that he could tend to the victims of the crash. On arriving at the scene, he found a motorcycle which had become united with the car it had struck. Some distance away lay the body of a young man, face down in a pool of blood. The meeting happened to be in a hospital that night, and a doctor also came rushing to the scene. The doctor rolled the body over to check for vital signs and, after finding a faint heartbeat, rushed back to the hospital to get more help. Due to the seriousness of the injuries, the young man had to be transported to a trauma center nearby. Lee stayed with the man until the ambulance arrived.

As Lee told his story, the entire meeting listened intently. Indeed, you could have heard a pin drop. The love of Lee for the victim could be felt by all.

While Lee waited for the ambulance, he took off his T-shirt and placed it under the young man's head. He then held him and began to pray. He pleaded with God to spare the young man's life. Finally the paramedics arrived and whisked the youth off to the trauma center where he remained in critical condition for several days.

I was hardly prepared for what was about to happen. Lee ended his story by saying that not only did the victim live today, he was actually in the meeting that night. He slowly turned until he was facing me, raised his arm, and pointed directly at me: "It's a miracle, youth enjoying sobriety my friend, because you're sitting right there."

A chill ran up my spine. I still had the bloodstained T-shirt, and now, in an AA meeting, I was to meet the man who had placed it under my head. I don't remember anything that was said afterward, but at the end of the meeting, I could hardly stand. When I did, you can be sure I embraced Lee with the fervor of a man well in the grips of a miracle. Suddenly I wanted to live!

Since this was not the first but the third near-fatal accident I'd been in, I came to believe that God had spared me for a reason. I realized that I am on this earth according to his schedule, not my own. When the time comes for me to die, I will die—and not a moment before then. And if I'm to live, the only way is to do it sober. Armed with this conviction, I decided to live my life to the best of my ability.

I returned home that night, opened the Big Book, and began reading. Although I had read it many times, the words now became meaningful, and had a clarity as never before. I figured out why I'd been unsuccessful with sobriety in the past. The answer was on page fifty-eight: "Those who do not recover are people who cannot or will not completely give themselves to this simple program ..." My problem was not that I could not, because I knew I could; my problem was that I would not. After this discovery, I commenced to follow the program as outlined in the Big Book, and for the first time in my life, I completely gave myself to this simple program.

Today I am pursuing the life of sobriety with the same eagerness I drank with. As a result of practicing the AA principles in all my affairs, I've found a life I never knew existed. I'm so overwhelmed with gratitude that there's no room for a bad day. Not only am I an active member of Alcoholics Anonymous, I'm an active member of the community as well. At last, I'm a man among men, a worker among workers, back in the mainstream of life. At twenty-seven, I have the brightest future imaginable, and it is all a result of what I found within the Fellowship of AA, the Big Book, and the love of a man who cushioned my head with the shirt off his back.

W. P.
COSTA MESA, CALIFORNIA

A DRUNK, PURE AND SIMPLE
JANUARY 2010

In San Francisco, in 1990, I was a lonely girl with a smile all sweet with pain. I was 29 years old and my life had begun unraveling years before. I had been struggling with my cocaine addiction for over a decade, attending CA, NA and AA meetings sporadically throughout the last three years, usually after particularly dark episodes of extended and voracious drug abuse. If only I could stop the drugs, I'd be fine. I was not willing, however, to give up drinking, as was suggested in all of my twelve-step meetings. I couldn't imagine life without alcohol. I did not announce myself as a newcomer at meetings, nor did I get a sponsor, work the Steps or follow any suggestions, except for one. I was a limbo girl who "kept coming back."

Everyone I knew drank and they drank more than I did, or so I thought. Never mind the hangovers, the blackouts, the morning shakes, the bruises on my body and my jaundiced eyes. I could drink with the best of them! Life was a party! And alcohol helped take the pain away.

I denied my alcoholism, but what I could not deny was how I felt alone, despairing and hopeless. Divorced and barely scraping by, I found myself bouncing from job to job, apartment to apartment, dysfunctional relationship to yet even more dysfunctional relationship, all the while riding the merry-go-round of drugs and alcohol.

I thought my childhood had something to do with all of this, so I made an appointment with a high-priced psychiatrist that I could not afford.

His office was in a ritzy part of town on a busy street lined with chic boutiques, trendy cafes and wine bars, a far cry from the seedy dives I now called home. I once worked on this same street, frequenting these bright and shiny places on my lunch hour or after work. Life was full of promise then. But at 19, I was a budding alcoholic and did not see what truly lay ahead: broken dreams left in the wake of insane intoxication.

Now I walked up the stairway to this doctor's office. I was prepared to reveal my stories of growing up in a home active with mental illness, fending for myself, the abusive relationships, and so on. I expected to lay back in a big leather couch as the good doctor took notes sympatheticly while nodding his head and eventually giving me the "magic cure" that would allow me to quit using drugs and be able to drink "normally."

This would not be the case. He asked me, first thing, "Why are you here?" I told him I had a drug problem and explained in detail my using history. He then asked me if I drank alcohol. "Yes, but that's not my problem," I said.

He asked me how often, how much and what happened when I drank. I answered honestly for the first time to anyone about my drinking, surprising even myself. He said "My dear, you have a problem with drugs and alcohol. You must realize that you must abstain from both completely."

He didn't want to hear about my past. He didn't want to psychoanalyze me. In fact he did not want to treat me at all, unless I got sober first. I was speechless. He asked me to pick up the phone, right then and there, and call the most radically intensive rehab program in the city at that time. I dialed the number as if in a trance. I remember my heart racing, my brain screaming silently, What on earth are you doing?

The phone rang for what seemed forever. Finally a woman answered. "What can I do for you?" she said. "I'm an alcoholic and a drug addict and I need help," I told her. "All of the counselors are in a meeting. Call back in an hour and someone will help you." Whew! Close call!

The doctor gave me his card, along with the phone number of the rehab and an AA meeting schedule. He suggested I get to meetings and we would take care of payment for his services after I stopped drinking. I couldn't get out of there fast enough. As I stepped into the world outside, I knew I was not ready to stop drinking.

I walked past the upscale bistros, sparkling and tinkling with sounds of laughter and clinking glasses. I stopped and peered inside for a moment. I saw well-dressed people sipping wine seemingly without a care in the world, certainly oblivious to me.

And then it hit me. The party was over. The party had been over for a long, long time. I couldn't drink like these people, all refined and civilized. I was a drunk, pure and simple. I was powerless over alcohol.

Thanks to this doctor, the seed had been planted. Up until then, my wall of denial kept me blaming everything and everyone else for my problems.

I wish I could say I sobered up right there and then. It took me another two years to surrender and fully comprehend that my life was unmanageable. I never did call that treatment center, which was probably a good thing. They considered twelve-step programs, Alcoholics Anonymous in particular, only a crutch. Upon completion of their program, clients were allowed to drink in moderation. I know today that would have never worked for me. I needed the spiritual solution so freely offered in Alcoholics Anonymous.

I continued to spiral, surviving my bottom and finding myself willing as only the desperate can be. My journey took me through two rehabs, a medical detox and eight months living in a womens' recovery home. I stayed sober through the program of Alcoholics Anonymous, attending meetings, working the Steps with a sponsor, participating in the Fellowship and doing service.

After about nine months of sobriety, I returned to the doctor to thank him for helping me. I came with a check to pay for the service he provided me that day, two years before. He refused and said my sobriety was payment enough.

JUDE H.
GRATON, CALIFORNIA

A HOMEGROWN DRUNK
MARCH 1995

On November 7, 1986 at four-thirty in the morning, a friend and I were returning home from bar-hopping all night in Lihue. I was drunk and stoned, and I missed a turn in Hanamaluu and drove off the road. My car flipped over several times, according to the police report, and came to rest near some trees. My best friend was thrown from the car, hit two trees, and was pronounced dead at the scene. I was taken to the hospital in shock but otherwise unhurt. I was released from emergency into the hands of the Kauai police who took me to the station, booked me for driving while intoxicated, and charged me with negligent homicide.

So there I was, twenty-five years old, in jail, and—having just caused the death of my best friend—facing ten years in prison. It was the lowest point in my life.

After four painful days in jail, I was released into supervised custody pending the trial. I was ordered to go to an AA meeting once a week at Serenity House and have court papers signed proving I was there. Well, I went to the meetings but I was still drinking and, amazingly, drinking and driving. I was scared about going to prison, and what would happen to me there, so I kept right on drinking to block my fears of getting beaten up, raped, or possibly killed. Two years of drinking and drugging later, after the trial and an appeal, I was sentenced to five years in Kauai Community Correctional Center. In September 1988, I went to prison. Although it wasn't what I imagined it would be, it still was an awful place.

I was born in 1961 in Lihue. My father was Filipino and my mother Hawaiian. I was a local boy all the way. Some local people think that alcoholism is a white man's disease brought from the mainland, but I am here to say that I'm an alcoholic and a drug addict and I was born and raised right here on Kauai. I started drinking by taking sips from my parents' drinks whenever I could. If my father asked me to get him a beer, I'd open it and take a few swallows on the way back to giving it to him. I'd also sneak swallows from mixed drinks sitting around on tables when my parents had people over. I never really got drunk, but I'd get a little buzz, enough to make me wonder what more alcohol could do.

I first started getting drunk in school. My friends and I'd get older classmates to buy the booze. There was always someone who knew where to get pot and we got drunk and stoned and went to the football games. If we were drunk enough, we'd try to start some trouble by hassling people. This went on all through high school every weekend, right up to graduation night when I made a total fool of myself in front of all my friends.

Soon after graduation, I moved to Oahu where I lived with relatives and got a job. I did most of my drinking at home since I was afraid I might go out of control if I drank in public. Then I made a few friends who just happened to be still in high school and went back to the drinking and drugging routine at football games. My job wasn't working out so I moved back to Kauai in 1983. I met up with my old friends from high school and when I wasn't working, I was partying all the time. I never kept jobs for very long because I was more interested in partying—drinking and smoking pot. I was always late for work and usually hung over and my attitude was that I didn't care. During this time, I realize now, I was very unhappy. My life was going nowhere. I had no prospects for the future. I couldn't keep a job long enough to advance. I was overweight and bloated from the drinking, and I didn't like myself.

It's unfortunate that it took an accident and the death of my friend to turn my life around, but that's what happened. While I was in prison, I started listening to one of my cellmates who was running the AA meeting inside. At first going to the meetings was just a way to relieve the boredom. Some of the guys only went to see the women. But by going to meetings I heard people describing how I was feeling. Some of these people had been where I had been and were now living what seemed to be happy lives without drinking or doing drugs. I decided to get a sponsor. I was able to get released to go to meetings on the outside and eventually, through good behavior and the work release program and the help of good counselors, I was released from prison after serving two years and four months.

I realized through AA that I had to change, and today my life is totally different. I no longer hang out with my old friends who are still drinking and using. If I see any of them I simply say a friendly hello and keep on going. I have new sober friends today and we engage in healthy activities. I'm playing volleyball, for example, and working out. I got my body in shape and I'm feeling better about myself than I have in a long, long time. I've had my present job for over a year (for eight months I actually held two jobs). I have goals now which include traveling and owning my own home. I've started getting back into my art work. Perhaps the best thing is that my relationships with family and friends have improved one-hundred percent. I'm glad to be alive today and possibly be able to help someone else who wants to get sober. If you are having a problem with your drinking and you want help, call AA. It works.

ANONYMOUS
KAUAI, HAWAII

WE FEEL THE SAME PAIN
JANUARY 1984

I am a 17-year-old, grateful, recovering alcoholic. When I came to Alcoholics Anonymous seventeen months ago, I was desperate, like so many of us who stumble through the doors of AA. Just being young doesn't mean we don't feel the same pain as older alcoholics, or our problems aren't as real.

I got involved with booze at a young age. I was a blackout drinker, and I drank alcoholically from the start. I also used drugs. So my progression was rapid.

Eventually, my "Go big or stay home" attitude got me into trouble–not to mention my mouth, and my lying, stealing, and conning. On binges, I would disappear for days. My parents, who had been enabling me, finally sought help. They could no longer predict or control my behavior, and neither could I. I was a wounded, sick bird determined to fly. And it was killing me!

My parents sent me to a drug and alcohol rehabilitation center, where I spent thirty-six days. People there gave me the tools, but I refused to use them. Information seeped into my brain, but that was as far as it went. I built no foundation, made no effort. Consequently, I got drunk.

What happened between the time I started to drink again and the day I came to AA is no mystery. I'm an alcoholic! Use your imagination–I'm not unique. But something was different now. The good times were gone.

Even though I was unhappy with my life, I had become accustomed to it. I knew how to act and react. It was easier to stay that way than it was to change. But somewhere along the road, the seed of AA had been planted. I couldn't go on living like the no-good rotten drunk I was. I was tired of waking up every morning and longing for the day to be over because I just didn't want to deal with it. The absolute worst was going to bed every single night with that tight, squeezing feeling in my chest. My heart was aching. I felt desperately alone. I needed help, and I knew it.

Not only did I admit and accept that I was alcoholic, but I then had to take responsibility for my recovery. When I first came to AA, I was resentful that I had come to the program so young. Today, I thank God that I have the chance to be whoever or whatever I want. You see, God gave me the choice–but I had to make it. He's been there to help me ever since.

I hope that more young people find Alcoholics Anonymous. It really is a beautiful program.

M. H.
LOCKPORT, NEW YORK

MOVING INTO THE FOURTH DIMENSION
AUGUST 1997

My name is Tony and I'm an alcoholic. I picked up my first drink at age thirteen. That's when my whole life changed. I was told later that I poured the last beer over my head, vomited, rolled in it, and walked home. My drinking never got much better after that.

Everything I ever cared about went on the back burner, like sports and education, while I hated anybody with any authority over me, like teachers, cops, parents. I got kicked out of school at fifteen and became a plumber full-time. I could drink like a fish the night before and still show up and do my job. My boss told me everybody wanted me for their helper because I worked hard. Three years later they weren't saying that anymore. I drank, went to work, and slept all day in a tub or in my car. Now my boss said that nobody wanted me for their helper. My reply was, "That's because they're all idiots."

I got picked up for drunk driving at age eighteen and had constant arrests for walking the streets aimlessly. I was drinking whiskey a lot and it wasn't strange for me to have a bottle of whiskey in one hand and a bottle of antacid in the other. I was starting to feel the physical effects of alcoholism, like ulcers, an enlarged liver, and hepatitis. I still thought there was a way I could drink in safety with a bad liver. I tried different drinks. I actually asked my friends if they would chip in for a liver transplant and they said no.

I'd try to control my drinking by going out later at night and I'd just get home later. I tried just doing drugs or just drinking. My mother brought a priest home and had him pray over me. Nothing worked. I could stop for three or four days, feel great, and then pick up that insane first drink and it would start all over again. I was losing my friends, and my family members were praying for me. They were all fed up.

One morning I was sitting in a local coffee shop, badly hung over, when I looked out the window and saw my old girlfriend, whom I hadn't seen in three years. She came in and I noticed something different about her. She was walking with her head up and her eyes were clear. She had a confidence about her which was not cockiness. I asked her, "Where the hell have you been?" She said, "In detox for thirty days and AA meetings every day after that." She proceeded to tell me about AA and then said, "You should give it a shot."

I tried to find some more fun in drinking and the next six months were hell. I drank alone because nobody wanted to baby-sit a drunk, and I woke up in the underground subway. It was total misery. My old girlfriend made my drinking even worse because now I knew there was a way out, and I was trying to ignore it.

I ended up in my first detox in January 1989—the day after Super Bowl Sunday. I spent five days there and got hope. I got out and went to my first AA meeting with an old friend of mine, and went to another meeting and another, and I kept seeing people I thought had fallen off the side of the earth. They said they'd been saving a seat for me and gave me the Big Book. I continued to go, but I never got active in the Fellowship. I had no home group, no Higher Power, no sponsor, and eventually I drank. I kept bounding in and out of AA, but I'd go to meetings drunk and they'd take me outside and talk to me to take me back to detox. Nobody said, "You're a nuisance or a pain in the neck"; they just said, "Keep coming," so I did.

Four or five detoxes later I got the gift of desperation. It was Thanksgiving 1989, and I was in detox and glad to be there, because I was sick and tired of being sick and tired. I was willing to do whatever AA wanted me to do. I had had enough. I got out on December 21, just in time for an alkathon (meetings around the clock on Christmas Eve and Christmas Day). I spent lots of time there. Then I joined a very active group that has a beginners meeting and a Twelve Steps and Twelve Traditions meeting and goes on four or five speaking commitments a week, including to jails and treatment facilities.

I got active in AA and got on my knees every morning, because I'd finally had enough and was open-minded and willing to try anything. I got a sponsor and he said, "Don't drink no matter what. Go to meetings, ask for help, and don't worry." He told me to never miss my group meeting unless I'm at a funeral—my own! I went to meetings every day for two years and made every commitment for two years. A little obsessive? Who cares—I didn't drink.

I couldn't help anybody in my early days, but I could give back by giving to my group, by making coffee and setting up. Things started to happen for me, like they gave me back my drivers license. I graduated from high school and I got my master's plumbing license—not bad at age twenty-nine. I made peace with my past, especially with my parents and brothers, and now we get along great. My father gave me my six-year medallion and my mother gave me my seven-year one.

I believe wholeheartedly in sponsorship. I sponsor some guys and they are a big part of what keeps me sober. They are gifts from God to me. I have two sponsors I use; one with twelve years who is also my best friend, and one with fifteen years who is extremely knowledgeable about AA. I really appreciate my friends, family, and work, because I try with the help of God and AA to work the Twelve Steps in every aspect of my life.

I met my wife on a white-water rafting trip, with all sober people. She was sober four years, I was two years, and we were both booking agents for our groups. After going out for two years, I set up a candle-light breakfast for us, and I asked her, "What are you doing for the rest of your life, one day at a time?"

"What do you mean?" she said.

I said, "Will you marry me?" She said, "Yes." That was three years ago and she truly is a gift from God. We both work the AA program to the best of our ability. As I write this, she is four months pregnant.

Just as it says in the Big Book: Sobriety is like being catapulted into the fourth dimension.

TONY A.
NORWOOD, MASSACHUSETTS

CHAPTER SEVEN

THE HEART OF IT—STEPS AND SERVICE

Service was the welcome mat to belonging;
the Twelve Steps were the key to living sober

"Today, the program of Alcoholics Anonymous for me is not just about going to meetings and conferences and meeting people and 'not drinking.' If I want to be happy in my sobriety, I absolutely need to work the Steps," writes the author of "Memoirs of a Conference Junkie."

The fun at a YPAA conference doesn't happen without months of service work beforehand. A young peoples' meeting will not stay open if no one does what needs to be done. The coffee won't be there if no one comes to the meeting hall early and starts it. Some members write about not seeing the benefit of service until they actually start doing it. Then the notion of service as drudgery tends to change. Service can be the welcome mat the young person needs to belong. When she's asked to bring the cookies or to be a greeter, she's suddenly a vital member of the group. And this service can be the prelude to Step work. It can keep a member coming back enough to want to start working the Steps.

"I didn't think service work had anything to do with solving my problem," an author writes. "When I was desperate enough to sweep the floor, I could listen to the other people who had been as desperate as I was." Adds the author of "Forever Young," "There is a large aspect of sociability in young peoples' activities, a much-needed counterweight to the isolation of alcoholism. But this only enhances their sponsorship and service work."

The AAs in this chapter talk about how vital the heart of the program is—working the Steps, passing it on, and keeping it all going with service work. "One day it will be left to the young people now in our Fellowship to carry on the original spirit and Traditions of AA," writes a member. "It will be up to us to teach newcomers how to maintain the type of sobriety that achieves the Promises of the Big Book."

CLUELESS
JANUARY 1997

I got sober in Minnesota—land of 10,000 treatment centers. My father had moved there four years earlier (when I was thirteen) and gotten sober. My mother had done just enough time in Al-Anon, before they divorced, to recognize my alcoholism. When Dad left, I started to experiment with alcohol and drugs. My parents had enough individual experience with the program that I was diagnosed immediately. They dogged me so much that I stopped for a while.

I'm an alcoholic, however, so that didn't last. I started up again at sixteen in earnest. A year later, I'd done time in three psych wards and jail. However, I never ended up in treatment. My judge nudged me into an evaluation that determined I belonged in an adolescent behavior modification ward.

My father reappeared at this time and made it clear that if I wanted him in my life, I'd have to stay sober. Moreover, he knew I'd have to go to weekly AA meetings. That would keep me sober, or at least abstinent. I went to just enough meetings to prove he was right. By not drinking, I was treating the body. By attending the meetings, I was treating the mind. I learned all about alcoholism without having experienced pitiful and incomprehensible demoralization of the spirit. Consequently, I developed a program that wasn't serious.

My dad's AA friends called me a treatment baby (even though I came from the psych ward, not a treatment center). There were lots of us teenagers in the program. Adolescent treatment was big business in Minneapolis.

I did the least amount of work possible to stay sober. I did whatever Step work I saw in front of me, but I wouldn't let myself see very much. Many of AA's Promises came true for me—superficially. But I really hadn't thoroughly worked Step One. At a deep level, I didn't believe I was an alcoholic. I really thought I could probably have just one drink.

But I didn't want to start over and lose my time, especially as I neared the ten-year mark. So I was superstitious about my program, but usually cavalier. While I knocked on wood every time I predicted future sobriety, I judged most AA folks as sicker than me. I figured that the "extracurricular" stuff was for them.

Extracurricular meant anything I didn't want to do—particularly service work. I didn't want to wash the cups or sweep the floors, so I never became part of the group. I never shook hands or brought donuts. Being GSR or serving on an H&I committee were definitely for alcoholics with nothing better to do. I thought those guys were especially sick.

With all my knowledge, somehow I'd missed it when someone said, "Read the Big Book." I never sat down and looked at it cover to cover; my copy still looked new. I'd been in enough Big Book meetings that I figured I'd heard the entire book. Besides, who had time for 164 boring, outdated pages? And those personal stories which went on forever! Hey, I had a life.

Of course the book sounded dull to me—I was listening to a room full of other alcoholics reading it. Instead, I could have studied it myself and identified—especially with the personal stories. I had no idea that my working of the Steps would be so enhanced if I became a part of the Fellowship—that it would place me in a position to hear about how to really work the Steps. I was truly clueless.

On my tenth AA birthday, I more or less went crazy. I probably should have been locked up, because I was dangerously vengeful and was having fantasies of murder. I'll spare you the details, but it's a wonder I didn't drink. It had taken ten years for my fundamental dishonesty, self-delusion, childishness, and selfishness to bring me to an emotional bottom.

Suddenly, the Steps and Promises were falling short. I wondered if AA was equipped to help me. I started going to therapy, but that didn't work. I had a whole new program to find, because I was spiritually miserable.

My new sponsor told me to get three meeting commitments. I didn't know what I was afraid of, but I hated the idea of being a greeter. Turns out it was great. In the past, I didn't have the time to bring donuts. But when I did, I was suddenly in the special crew of people who put on the meeting. I was becoming a part of the group.

For years I'd noticed that people with more time than me were absent here and there. I'd assumed they were slacking off, so I did too. What I found on my new adventure was that they had other AA commitments. When I missed Joe with twenty-five years on Sunday morning, I thought he slept in. Then I showed up at a GSR meeting and there he was. I thought Mary with sixteen years blew off Monday night once a month, but then I ran into her at the H&I committee meeting.

I didn't think service work had anything to do with solving my problem, because I hadn't done the service work to find out. When I did, it changed my life. When I was desperate enough to sweep the floor, I could listen to the other people who had been as desperate as I was.

So now I'm on the lookout for young people like me. I hope that before they crash sober they'll find the solution that I found just in time.

ANONYMOUS

FOREVER YOUNG
FEBRUARY 2010

In parts of Southern California, it's not uncommon for 13-, 14-, 15- and 16-year-old boys and girls simply to walk into AA meetings. There are about 25 active young peoples' committees in California, busily showing thousands of young AAs that recovery involves service and having fun without drinking. Still, according to our latest membership survey, in 2007 only 2.3 percent of AA members were under 21 years old.

Although AA has long had young people as members, they usually weren't as young or as numerous as today. Co-founder Bill W. wrote

about the first young person to join AA: "Then from another quar-
ter we turned up with a prize. I guess this was the beginning of AA's
young people's department. This new one, Ernie, had been a terribly
wild case, yet he caught on very quickly to become AA number four."
(*Alcoholics Anonymous Comes of Age,* p. 73). Ernie was 30 years old at
the time, July 1935, a scant month after co-founder Dr. Bob's last drink
led to the formation of AA. The Big Book, published in 1939, states,
"Several of our crowd, men of thirty or less, had been drinking only a
few years, but they found themselves as helpless as those who had been
drinking twenty years." (*Alcoholics Anonymous,* p. 33) Obviously, men
in their 20s tried to get sober in our Fellowship during the 1930s.

Recently I flipped through some old national AA directories, looking for early young peoples' groups. I found a Cleveland, Ohio, "Young
Peoples' Group" from February 1945. In August 1946 the "Thirty-Five
and Under Group" of Philadelphia, Pa., first appeared.

By February 1948, the National Directory included eight young
peoples' groups in Cleveland, Philadelphia, San Diego (a mens' group
and a womens' group), Los Angeles, New York City, Pittsburgh and
Detroit. Young peoples' groups had been firmly established.

As a newcomer, I attended a "20-40 Group" for a while; people had
to be between 20 and 40 years old to participate in the meeting.

At my first young peoples' convention, I somehow summoned the
courage to ask a young woman I barely knew to dance with me on Saturday night. This was a slow dance, making my nervousness, sweating and clumsy moves even more noticeable. After enduring this for
a while, she looked up at me ever so sweetly and said, "You're really
very light on my feet!" We both laughed, and I got out of myself long
enough to enjoy the rest of the evening. At that time, I never would
have danced to unfamiliar music in a roomful of older people.

There is a large aspect of sociability in young peoples' activities, a
much-needed counterweight to the isolation of alcoholism. But this
only enhances their sponsorship and service work. And young peoples'
conventions leave a positive impact in their wake. The energy sur-
rounding the 1965 Long Beach ICYPAA led to a young peoples' club-

house in the San Diego beach area. In 1971 a group from San Diego attended the ICYPAA in Reno, Nev., and upon their return started a young peoples' group that to this day routinely has 75 people at its Friday night meeting. The 1973 ICYPAA in San Francisco sparked the formation of ACYPAA. The 1983 ACYPAA committee in San Diego morphed into the Greater San Diego Young People in AA Committee.

Young AAs think nothing of driving 15 hours on Friday, sleeping en masse on someone's floor, attending a Saturday event, then turning around on Sunday and driving back in time for school or work. I've done it myself. Thus the young peoples' groups establish strong personal ties by speaking at each other's groups and supporting each other's activities. Now there are young peoples' AA conventions in Canada, Australia, South Africa, Sweden and other international locations. Europe is preparing to host its first young peoples' convention in 2010. Many young people in AA save their money and vacation time so they can travel to other states and countries to support their young peoples' activities. This state-to-state and now country-to-country sponsorship of young peoples' activities is in the best tradition of Twelfth Step work.

Members of young peoples' groups from the 1940s would likely be astonished at the extent of today's YPAA activities. I hope that 60 years from now, when today's young people are the white-haired elder statesmen and women of AA, they, too, will be astonished by the ever-expanding, creative Twelfth Step work of new generations of young people.

ANONYMOUS
CALIFORNIA

YOUNG PEOPLE IN SERVICE
DEAR GRAPEVINE, NOVEMBER 2008

The camaraderie and fellowship I have found through young peoples' AA groups in the past year have been monumental in my sobriety. And the International Conference of Young People in AA (ICYPAA) weekend in Oklahoma City this past July smashed the delusion that I need to be intoxicated to enjoy friendship and to weather the hardships of daily life.

Another delusion that ICYPAA brought crumbling down was the idea that young people are about having fun to the point of being oblivious to general service. Nothing could be further from the truth.

ANONYMOUS
INDIANAPOLIS, INDIANA

MEMOIRS OF A CONFERENCE JUNKIE
MARCH 2000

I grew up in the program of Alcoholics Anonymous, an experience for which I am truly grateful. When I quit drinking in 1991, I was seventeen years old and had no clue what teenagers did besides break rules and make bad choices for themselves. I went to meetings where people older than I was told me they spilled more beer on their tie than I ever drank. This grew tiresome, and I often found it difficult to relate to people who shared about typical consequences related to their drinking—things such as bankruptcy, divorce, losing children or jobs, repeated DWIs, or getting kicked out of bars.

Nonetheless, all of us who recover young eventually realize that despite the different situations, the feelings are usually the same. I discovered that the choices that I make today have a tendency to determine what happens to me in the future, and taking action in my recovery is imperative if I want to learn how to live happily in sobriety. I would like to say that I immediately obtained a sponsor and worked the Steps and my life immediately improved, but that would not be entirely true. I did, however, get involved with service work, which was my saving grace at the time.

As I recall, my first exposure to any large scale AA gathering occurred at the 1993 Flagstaff Roundup, 140 miles north of my home in Phoenix. This was the first time I allowed myself to dance in the presence of other people without being under the influence of alcohol. Less than one week later, I found myself in Tucson at the first annual Arizona State Conference of Young People in Alcoholics Anonymous (referred to as ASCYPAA). This event has played a vital role in my life for several reasons. Although I didn't then understand the significance of doing service work in order to maintain my spiritual growth, I was able to recognize the importance of the host committee in relation to organizing the event. I was overwhelmed by the end result at the Saturday night speaker meeting, as I was surrounded by hundreds of enthusiastic young people excited about being sober. I was profoundly moved.

At the time, my exposure to young peoples' AA consisted of a Saturday afternoon meeting called Green Eggs and Ham and a Friday late night candlelight meeting that often ran until after one in the morning, followed by coffee at a nearby diner until the sun rose. Then Phoenix was selected to host the second ASCYPAA the following year, and eager to get involved with the ASCYPAA scene, I attended the meeting in which the committee was to be elected to carry out various tasks related to hosting the conference. Much to my dismay, however, I was not nominated for any "important" positions. With my fragile ego bruised, I left resentful. A friend of mine, on the other hand, got involved with the outreach committee, and endured my harassment as he made announcements of pre-conference events and monthly speaker meetings and dances every week at our Monday meeting. Meanwhile, the young peoples' movement boomed throughout the Phoenix Valley with the formation of a few new young peoples' meetings and a host committee meeting every other week to plan the upcoming conference.

By 1994, the thought occurred to me that it might be kind of cool to have the young peoples' conference in Mesa the next year. I solicited a couple of other friends to form a bid committee and began one of the most interesting experiences in my sobriety. When we were awarded the conference, we were on top of the world. I had never been trusted to do anything "important," much less in the capacity of hosting a state conference. My Higher Power kept my ego in check though, and that year I learned more about the Twelve Traditions and about general responsibility than any other time I can remember.

But near the end of the year, I was asked to resign from my position due to the fact that I often failed to complete assignments—usually something as simple as making a flyer. I suddenly became aware of the fact that since I hadn't thoroughly worked the Steps as outlined in the Big Book, I had nothing other than my position on the committee to keep me coming back. Overwhelmed with loneliness and fear, I called my sponsor, and we started working the program of Alcoholics Anonymous versus merely partaking in the fellowship. The committee allowed me to stay on and I eventually learned how to follow through with my responsibilities.

We successfully hosted ASCYPAA '95 in Mesa and today, ASCYPAA is gearing up for its seventh consecutive year. The Valleywide Young Peoples' AA meeting list has forty meetings listed per week, including two regularly attended Big Book studies and a roving Twelve Traditions and Twelve Concepts study on Sunday nights. A new generation of young people is coming in and according to our Area Delegate, "Our future looks good!"

Today, the program of Alcoholics Anonymous for me is not just about going to meetings and conferences and meeting people and "not drinking." If I want to be happy in my sobriety, I absolutely need to work the Steps. If alcohol is but a symptom of my disease, that means the problem is me and the choices that I make for myself. If change doesn't happen within me, I will continue to do the same things. The Twelve Steps are a means for this change to occur and are absolutely vital if I want to stay alive.

MIKE S.
PHOENIX, ARIZONA

MORE THAN ONE WAY
FEBRUARY 2010

One of the common misconceptions about Young People in Alcoholics Anonymous (YPAA) conventions and committees is that they are separate from AA as a whole, serve only to isolate young members of AA from the general body, and exclude the general body from their events. This couldn't be further from the truth. A large reason that YPAA is in existence is so younger members can see that there are many people their own age who are getting and staying sober in AA.

While many younger AAs attend conventions and events and never participate in the committees that organize these events, there is still value in merely attending. Conventions and committees help advance our primary purpose: to carry the message to the still sick and suffering alcoholic. Panels at YPAA conventions focus on the Steps and Traditions, as well as other recovery topics such as relationships; carrying the message into hospitals, treatment centers and correctional institutions; long-term sobriety; or the AA slogans.

A recent ICYPAA in Oklahoma City featured the first Young Peoples' Forum, an all-day event sponsored by the General Service Office.

Serving on YPAA committees has given me the opportunity to work with members of AA to put on a convention. Through this committee work, I have learned how to place principles before personalities, begun to understand that it's okay for me to be wrong, and that it is also all right for me to allow others to be wrong and to make mistakes. Learning to let go is a huge part of service work on all levels. Another benefit of committee work is the outreach that YPAA stresses at all levels: local, area, regional and, in some cases, national.

Younger members can see that there are people their own age getting sober in AA.

My YPAA experience opened me up to a whole new world of service and helped further my understanding of the service structure. There isn't one "right" way to carry the message. Some people need to get involved in YPAA to see how important general service is to AA. Others, like myself, needed YPAA to enhance my already existing journey in general service.

DAVE S.
CLEVELAND, OHIO

Y.E.S., Y.E.S., Y.E.S.
DEAR GRAPEVINE, MAY 2003

I just wanted to thank you for the department called "Youth Enjoying Sobriety (Y.E.S.)." I bring an institutions meeting into an alcohol rehabilitation center for teens aged twelve to eighteen. Although many of these beautiful recovering drunks knew they were powerless over alcohol, many felt terminally unique due to the misconception that they were too young to be part of our Fellowship. Bringing them back issues of the Grapevine and pointing out the "Youth Enjoying Sobriety" department showed them there were young people like themselves all over the world who were also in recovery, and that the "we" in our First Step really was big enough to include them.

DAYANN M.
OZONE PARK, NEW YORK

TALK ABOUT BRIDGING THE GAP
JANUARY 2009

It was right about my one-year sobriety birthday and I was wallowing in fear and self-pity. Some kids from the Indiana Conference for Young People in AA (INCYPAA) swooped me up and made me a committee member. I had no car, was dependent on my father to take me to meetings and events, and was petrified of commitment. The second time I showed up at one of their outings, the chairman, whom I have come to love dearly, informed me that I was now a committee member. Car or no car, someone would make sure I was at their meetings and events.

One of the many service opportunities I have been blessed to participate in came via another insistent friend in the program. Our intergroup chair pointed out to me that as young people in recovery we ought to be looking to outreach to other young people who were still suffering. INCYPAA decided to take a meeting into a juvenile treatment center every Wednesday for a month. That was four months ago, and I can't even begin to relate the warmth that working with these kids has brought to all of our hearts.

We invited Area 23's Treatment Facility Committee chair to accompany us for our initial visit and share a bit of experience with us.

She did, and it was quite a meeting! Most of these kids are cross-addicted and some of them don't even refer to alcohol when they share. After a short reading from a Grapevine article on getting sober young, we started to go around the circle.

I was mortified as these kids shared their experiences with trying to obtain and maintain sobriety. They kept talking about drugs and alcohol. No, I thought. What is this Area TFC chairwoman, who's been sober for more than twenty years, going to say? What of AA's singleness of purpose? The time came for her to share, and I braced myself for the chewing-out I knew was coming. She shared her story; she said that drugs had been in her past, but in the end it was alcohol that had brought her to her knees.

At heart she was an alcoholic, first and foremost, and because of that she had come to know sobriety through AA. Wow.

And so began a weekly journey that most of us would not trade for the world. We don't preach or educate; we share our experience, strength, and hope.

In recent days, these kids have started showing up at some of our home group meetings.

One of my best friends is now a proud sponsor of a girl who recently graduated from the facility. Talk about bridging the gap!

We can only hope that these new young members realize a few things: they never have to pick up another drink, one day at a time; they never have to be alone again; and they have brought more joy and appreciation to our sobriety than they could ever imagine.

JASON P.
CARMEL, INDIANA

FOUNTAIN OF YOUTH
AUGUST 1998

ight months ago I came back to the community where I got sober to find that my former home group had almost completely fallen apart. I walked back in that first Wednesday night to find three newcomers just sitting around talking to each other. A little after seven, when the meeting was scheduled to begin, I asked them who was chairing. They told me that there hadn't been a business meeting in months and that nobody really had jobs. I asked them where the group format was and they told me that they had never seen one. I didn't like what I was hearing and seeing; I couldn't believe how far apart this group had grown in just two years.

Eleven years ago when I first came to an AA meeting, this was where I had come. In 1989, when I finally decided that it was really time to do the work to stay sober, this was the group that I joined. This young peoples' group had been like a second family to me; my older sister had been one of its founding members three years before I got sober. This was where I learned about recovery, where I made my first real friendships, where I learned how to have fun without drinking, where I was taught how to live sober. I had watched this group of young people change a lot of lives. As far as I was concerned, this group was where we had saved one another's lives. But no one had stuck around to make sure that it was here to save the next person. That hurt me.

I was aware that many of the old group had moved away or gone back out, but I knew of at least a few who were still in the area who could have been there to show this group how it works, to extend the hand of AA. Where were they? This was the one young peoples' group in at least a thirty miles radius and there was not one young person with long-term sobriety who could show up for it? I couldn't understand. It felt very wrong to me—this was not what our program was meant to be like. At least this isn't the way I learned it; I was taught that you have to give it away to keep it.

Sad and frustrated, I rummaged through the boxes in the corner of the hall. I found our group's binder—no format, no chips, and there hadn't been an entry in the notebook since 1995. I winged it. I had come for a meeting and so had these three kids. I did what the drunks who came before me taught me how to do; I took responsibility and I passed on the message.

After we had closed with the Serenity Prayer, I let the guys know that I was committed to getting this group going again. I asked them to spread the word that the Young Peoples' Meeting was back. I volunteered to chair for the rest of the month and we decided to hold a business meeting the following week to draw up a new group format.

I drove the twenty minutes home that night feeling very full of all of the best that this program promises us, if we are willing to do the work: success, hope, serenity, joy, satisfaction. And that was only the beginning. In these last few months our group has come together in an amazing way. We put in a bid for the New England Young Peoples' Conference, we traveled to Syracuse for the Great Lakes Conference, we are going out on commitments. Two weeks ago I watched a sixteen-year-old girl with five months speak for her first time. She set the room afire and she walked away with a whole new feeling about herself and her recovery. And as a result, so did I.

We now have monthly business meetings, we have jobs and people to show up for them, we are sharing the true joys of Unity, Service, and Recovery. Best of all, at least for me, this last Wednesday night there wasn't an empty seat in the room, there wasn't enough time for everyone to speak, and I had the pleasure of witnessing both white chips and a two-year medallion being given to members of my home group.

Having the opportunity to watch this program work in young peoples' lives the way that it worked in mine is one of the greatest joys of my sobriety. It is an immeasurable gift and I didn't have to do anything special to receive it; I simply took what I was taught and passed it on.

I show up early, I am involved, and I reach my hand out to the next person coming through the door. It's amazing how very easy it is to make a difference for others and for yourself just by accepting the responsibility to pass the message on.

HEIDI T.
NELSON, NEW HAMPSHIRE

WE WHO ARE NEXT IN LINE
SEPTEMBER 1994

I am a twenty-two-year-old alcoholic. After several years of hard drinking I was dying of alcoholism. Doctors had told me I was incurable and hopeless. I began to recover through the program of Alcoholics Anonymous, and by the grace of a very loving God and AA I'm still sober three years later. Because of my recovery I was allowed to pursue a lifelong dream and I enlisted in the Air Force. This has given me the opportunity to attend AA meetings in different states and other nations and I have noticed something interesting in my travels. Where a meeting allows people to talk about drug addiction, it usually allows them to talk about everything else under the sun, and they invariably do. In these meetings that have little regard for AA Traditions there seem to be more people who go back to drinking, more people who don't practice the Twelve Steps, more people who don't have (or don't use) a sponsor, more people who don't extend a safe welcome to visitors or pay much attention to newcomers.

However, on the other side of the coin, meetings that insist on discussing subjects related to recovery from alcoholism only—and stand by it—are often meetings that make sure a new person is welcomed and given phone numbers with maybe a pamphlet or two, meetings that make their visitors feel like they've come home, meetings that get involved with hospitals and institutions committees and their service centers. These meetings produce a different result. The old-timers are there, and they have a respected voice because of their tested experience. People at those meetings have and use sponsors and they talk about how they've applied the AA program in their daily lives. They have more solutions and talk less about problems, more peace and less turmoil, and more people who stay recovered and less who go back to drinking again.

Bill W. was right: AA cannot fix the world. AA's Twelve Steps and Traditions can be applied universally to everyone's benefit, but AA itself must forever remain by and for alcoholics. To mix up our primary purpose—freedom from alcohol—with drug addiction and overeating and other destructive dependencies erodes the unity that binds us together, unity we must keep to survive. It's not a matter of exclusivity, it's a matter of the survival of AA's very existence.

Since the Fellowship's early days we have had the Twelve Steps to guide us. But the bedrock of AA has always been one drunk talking to another. Through this, the depth of understanding is reached that gives hope to a desolate alcoholic's heart. One drunk to another—not one addict to an alcoholic or one codependent to an alcoholic. One drunk to another drunk.

One day it will be left to the young people now in our Fellowship to carry on the original spirit and Traditions of AA, even though the buzz words and trends will come and go. It will be up to us to teach newcomers how to maintain the type of sobriety that achieves the Promises of the Big Book and dispels some of the fables of recovery popular today. It will be up to us to help the newcomer from the street dry out, shakes and pukes and all. We will be left to teach the little things: how to sit at the front, not the back of the room, say hello to the new guy, wash coffee cups and ashtrays. One day it will be up to us to uphold the Traditions. It will be up to us to keep it simple.

Today, young people are learning from the last generation of AAs who got the message straight from the original old-timers. We must be diligent in preserving the AA way of life through our actions and our participation at meetings amid an ever growing attitude of "I come first" rather than "sobriety comes first." There are many catchwords, but only one program of recovery outlined in the Big Book.

Old-timers, there are still some of us who desperately need you and value what you have to say.

Young people, it's our responsibility to follow in their footsteps.

JENIFER C.
BURY ST. EDMUNDS, ENGLAND

CHAPTER EIGHT

LIVING LIFE, GROWING UP

Through good times and bad, these AAs turn to the Fellowship
and their Higher Powers and keep going

"The gifts of sobriety have already begun to blow my mind," writes the author of a letter to Dear Grapevine.

Suddenly the worst is over. We've gotten sober, worked the Steps and begun to grow up—what a concept! Some of us ride the pink cloud for a while. We have friends and life is beautiful.

Then the pink cloud vanishes into vapor and we crash to earth. The worst is back! The problems and emotions once covered over with alcohol are popping to the surface. There could be marriage issues, trouble with school, a wife's illness. Heartbreak and divorce. Depression. Layoffs.

And then life is beautiful again—a new job, a new house, a new romance.

"I found a new life in AA, a life filled with challenge, promise, and hope," the author of "Sober in the Sixties" writes. "There have been many times when I've felt inadequate to meeting life's demands, but AA and the Twelve Steps have always helped me find a way."

"There have been times in my sobriety when I started to feel sorry for myself. Not so much because I am not able to drink, but because I always have to be responsible for my actions," a member writes in "Living Large." "I think to myself, teenagers/young people are supposed to do stupid things, and because I have a program, I can't! But looking back, I can truthfully say that I have made plenty of mistakes in my sober life. In fact, probably the only mistake that I haven't made is that I haven't picked up a drink—yet."

The good and the bad. Young AAs slowly learn acceptance. Life goes on.

"There have been painful times, happy times, fearful times, and glorious times," says the author of "Growing Pains." "The enjoyment of life on a more mature basis more than compensates for the pain."

LIVING LARGE
MARCH 2006

'm twenty-nine years old, and by the grace of God, I have been sober since May 19, 1990. Sometimes that feels like forever, while other times it feels as if it is only yesterday. I still have a lot to learn.

I grew up in the suburbs with a loving family. At age three, I was diagnosed with cerebral palsy. The doctors told my parents that their youngest son might never be able to ride a bicycle, learn to swim, or graduate from high school.

I look back now and see that I used that as an excuse to not try to reach my potential. As I grew up, I had very little self-esteem and few problem-solving skills. I started to feel more and more like an outsider. Why should anyone else care for me when I didn't even like myself? When alcohol came into my life, I took to it very fast. I never really crossed the line into alcoholism—when I started out, I was already past that line.

Whenever the media covers a shooting at a school, my reaction is just like everyone else's: I'm shocked at today's youth. Then I have to remember that it could have been me. I remember being in grade school and carrying around weapons, or having parties in the eighth grade where people would fire handguns from my parents' backyard. When I was ten years old, I broke a classmate's neck. I was on a first-name basis with the youth officer in my town because my friends and I had so many encounters with him. All in all, my life was not normal, and I earned my seat at the tables of AA. I wish I could tell a very elaborate bottoming-out story, but the truth is much more simple. I got caught drinking, and it doesn't take much more than that to get a fourteen-year-old kid in serious trouble.

For someone in my situation, an inpatient hospital stay is the easiest way to make a "geographic change." While in the treatment center, I found AA. Where would I be now if those AA members didn't volunteer their time to bring meetings into hospitals?

When I went to my first meeting, I didn't see anybody who looked like me, but these fellow AA members told me what happened to them and what it was like now. I can't say that I really wanted what they had, but I knew that I didn't want what I had. So I kept coming back.

Throughout the years, I got noticed a lot because of my age and length of sobriety. Statements were directed toward me, such as, "It is so great that you are sober at such a young age," or "You can help other young people better than I can." It didn't seem like any of the other hard work I did, such as working the Steps, was even acknowledged. I grew to resent the attention that I received because of my youth.

I will be thirty soon, and now I'm not always the youngest person at the meeting. My uniqueness has been slipping away. Where am I now in AA?

Well, I have worked the Twelve Steps a couple of times. I have chaired committees at both district and area level. I have told my story to groups ranging from one alcoholic to an audience of several thousand, and it has been published in AA literature. I have sponsored dozens of alcoholics. I am no longer seen as a young person, but rather as a trusted servant. I have become a member among members. I finally believe that I truly belong here.

There have been times in my sobriety when I started to feel sorry for myself. Not so much because I am not able to drink, but because I always have to be responsible for my actions. I think to myself, Teenagers/young people are supposed to do stupid things, and because I have a program, I can't! But looking back, I can truthfully say that I have made plenty of mistakes in my sober life. In fact, probably the only mistake that I haven't made is that I haven't picked up a drink—yet.

I used to put expectations on myself that were just not necessary. I felt that because I was living a sober life, there were things that I wasn't able to do. I never went to any of my high school proms for fear that there would be drinking there. I thought I was doomed to a life filled with only AA dances and picnics. It took me a long time to find out that

AA wasn't here to limit my life, it was here to fulfill it.

In the past fifteen years that I have been in AA, I have attended dozens of concerts and weddings, gone on vacations, and gone to nightclubs. I have become a firefighter, a black belt in judo, a scuba diver, a skydiver, and a motorcyclist. I graduated from the college of my choice, and I was able to study in Europe for a semester. I have a good job, I own my own home, and I have great credit. In May, I married the most beautiful, kind, loving woman in the world on a beach in Maui. Not bad for a little kid who was never expected to ride a bicycle, right?

Today I understand that I go to AA to live my life, not live my life to go to AA. So, when anyone asks me what a young sober member of AA can do for fun, I always tell him or her, "With the exception of drinking, you can do anything legal." It is a big world out there with tons of possibilities to explore.

When I meet my maker someday, it will not matter how long I was sober or how young I was. Nor will it matter what life experiences I have had, or the size of my bank account. What I want to be judged on is how good a husband, and possibly a father, I was. Did I love and support others as much as God loved and supported me? Today it is no longer about who cares for me, it is about learning to love others. Without the principles of Alcoholics Anonymous, I would not be able to live the life that God wanted me to.

KEVIN P.
SCHAUMBURG, ILLINOIS

GROWING PAINS
JULY 1969

My first encounter with my addictive personality came on my fifteenth birthday. I was in the hospital; the diagnosis was "nervous condition"; the treatment was morphine and tranquilizers. Very quickly I learned to produce agonizing headaches to keep those needles and pills coming. But my physician soon caught on. I was withdrawn from the drugs and sent home with a bottle of sugar pills. I had overheard the plot, and I wondered why on earth the doctor would do such a thing.

From that time until AA, I was a part-time hypochondriac. I say part-time because making good grades, caring what people thought, and wanting to be somebody became more important to me than playing the "sick" game.

In my senior year of high school, I started dating my husband-to-be. He was eight years older than me and well into his drinking problem. After our marriage, we both threw ourselves into working hard, and drank only on weekends. We had a comfortable home and lots of friends, and were known as "that nice young couple." To round out this beautiful picture, a girl child was born. Then, during the third year of our marriage, my husband lost his job and accepted another one that took us to Thailand. We were making more money than I had ever dreamed possible.

After two years of hard drinking, pill-taking, and hospitalization for operations, I came back to the United States. I had lost thirty pounds; I had blood poisoning and a myriad of other physical problems. I was hospitalized for about six weeks and put back together physically. I knew I was emotionally and physically ill, but I did not know I was an alcoholic. My doctor told me I must change my pattern of living or I would not have much longer to live. I don't remember consciously asking for help, but I started wanting to get well. An AA member suggested I try Al-Anon. There I was told that if I was to get anything out of the program I should give up all chemicals. I asked the Higher Power and called on the strength of the group to help me do this. I have been free of all chemical crutches ever since, one day at a time.

Exactly one year after my arrival at Al-Anon, I was behind the podium in an AA group, admitting I was an alcoholic.

There have been painful times, happy times, fearful times, and glorious times. Growing pains are sometimes hard to bear, but the enjoyment of life on a more mature basis more than compensates for the

pain. This month I am twenty-nine years old and almost five years sober. I am still trying to reach new levels of honesty and higher spiritual
dimensions and most of all to know the truth and be rid of ego.

P. A. K.
AMARILLO, TEXAS

SNAPSHOTS OF SOBRIETY
MAY 1999

I got sober in November 1980 at the age of fifteen, and during the
summer of 1991, when I'd just graduated from college, I traveled
alone to Florence, Italy to visit family members for a month. My
father had come to America from Italy at the age of twenty-one, having met my mother while she was in Italy attending school. After
visiting Italy with my father some years before, this trip was something I wanted to do alone, something like a challenge. I wrote in
my journal often during the flights and while waiting for my con-
nections, thanking God for the opportunity to travel. It was truly an
adventure for me to be all alone and going across the ocean to visit
family members I hardly knew.

I arrived at the small Florence airport with only a few hours of sleep
and severe jet lag, but I was very excited to see everyone. My aunt and
cousin were there to greet me. It was a great visit. We enjoyed getting to know each other, spending time walking through the center of
town, going to museums and shopping. My grandmother loves to cook
and we ate some wonderful Italian meals. Most everyone would drink
wine at lunch and dinner. They would offer me a glass, and tempting
as it looked, I knew the right answer was "No, thank you." I also knew
it would be a good idea to look for a meeting, so after spending a few
days with my family, I checked the phone book for AA and found the
number listed. The woman I talked to was very helpful and told me the
meetings were at the American Church on Via Rucellai, near the train

station. I hopped on a bus the next day and found my way there.

I will never forget ringing the bell at the gate and walking down the gravel drive to the door that opened on a staircase going down. In the basement I found about forty-five people waiting for the meeting to begin. As I started talking to some of them I felt right at home. It is the most incredible feeling to come in from the streets of a foreign country, where they do not speak English and they drink lots of wine, and suddenly feel so welcomed by a room full of sober people.

I soon discovered why there were so many people at this meeting. That year the World AIDS Conference was being held in Florence. Most of the people were involved with the conference. Some of them were HIV positive and others were not. It was a very powerful meeting, and the thing I remember most about that day was that all of us were present, living in the moment and celebrating life, sober. After the meeting several of us went for pizza at a little place near San Marco Square.

I only spent one afternoon with these people, but I took home with me a lifetime of love. When I look back at the pictures from that day, I have a smile in my heart and I thank God for AA and for the gift of sobriety.

I'm thirty-three years old now and the mother of one-year-old twins! Since that trip I have returned to Italy several times to visit my family. Knowing my situation, they no longer offer me the glass of wine, but I still look forward to the meeting at the American Church on Via Rucellai where I fondly remember my friends from the summer of '91.

JILL L.
OMAHA, NEBRASKA

DIGGING MY BOTTOM
MARCH 2010

Once at my home group I heard a good friend talk about the meaning of HOPE. He used the acronym Hearing Other Peoples' Experience. This has really stuck to me. Everything I go through, I know that at least one of my friends in the program has gone through. Listening and being able to relate to people in the program has been a big part of my sobriety.

I started experimenting at a very young age. I can't recall my first drink but I know I was young and that alcohol was easy to get because my parents drank. By the time I was 13 I was drinking every weekend and a few times a week before and/or after school.

I always remember feeling different from the people I drank with. I would watch others drink and when they started getting too drunk they would stop. I would drink until I blacked out or passed out, whichever came first. I loved the way alcohol made me feel. I felt prettier, older or cooler, and nothing mattered. By the age of 15 I had some kind of mind-altering substance in my body at all times, numbing the pain. I was running away on a regular basis, my mom never knew where I was, and I was living the life of a true loser. I had lost all love and respect I ever had for myself. I didn't think my life was worth any more than the way I was already living.

When I think about how badly I hurt myself and my family, I always remember the time when I was crying to my mom about a fight I'd had earlier with my boyfriend. I had been on one of my runaway binges and hadn't slept in days. My mom brought me something to drink, and I drank some and it went down my windpipe. I was so weak that I could not even cough to get the fluid out. I couldn't breathe. My mom started crying and said, "Breathe, Abbie, breathe!" I was finally able to take a breath. I was so scared. I was afraid to die, but at the same time I was afraid to live.

That did not stop me, though. I kept digging my bottom for a few more months. On Nov. 26, 2002, I went to a meeting with my brother, who was already in recovery. I had been sober for two days because my boyfriend and I decided we were going to straighten our lives up. When I walked in the room I remember feeling a comfort I had never felt before. All they wanted was for me to stay sober and to "keep coming back."

When I got into the rooms of Alcoholics Anonymous, I didn't think I was going to stay sober. I just wanted the pain to go away. I did what you guys suggested and I went to meetings, got a sponsor and worked the Steps. My life started to change.

Okay, now for the HOPE part of this story. I am only 23 years old and I am living a life beyond my wildest dreams, with over six years of sobriety. I have completely grown up in the program of Alcoholics Anonymous. Thanks to the people in the rooms, I think of myself as a woman and I respect myself today. Everything in my life today I owe to the program of Alcoholics Anonymous. Because of the program and support from other AAs, I went back to school, got my GED, and even attended some college. I met my husband in Alcoholics Anonymous, and when we got married, 50 percent of the people at our wedding were recovering alcoholics. My husband and I had our first child almost a year ago, and I am able to be a mom today and to feel love that I never thought was possible with my daughter and husband. I could go on and on about the blessings that Alcoholics Anonymous has given me

ABBIE T.
HURRICANE, UTAH

SOBER IN THE SIXTIES
JULY 2006

was born on June 29, 1945. I was born again on the date of my last drink: May 26, 1964. I was eighteen years old, homeless, and scared. I didn't find AA. It found me. Here's how it happened.

My father allowed me and my two-year-old daughter to live in an old travel trailer in Rosarito Beach, Mexico. It had no electricity, no running water, and no toilet facilities. I spent my days recovering from the night before while looking for someone—anyone—to watch my little girl so I could go into Tijuana to drink and party till dawn. I could not sleep, but I could drink until I passed out, only to wake a few hours later shaking and anxious. I had pills for that and if I got too relaxed, I had pills for that, too. I felt like a failure and chastised myself for being an unfit mother.

One night, after a near-disastrous ride back to the beach from Tijuana, I stood on the cliff outside my tiny trailer and prayed for the first time in years. It was a simple prayer, one most of us AAs are familiar with: "God, if there is a God, please help me."

The following morning I went to a nearby cantina to get food for my baby and, of course, a drink for myself. After becoming well-lubricated, I introduced myself to two men seated at a table, and was astounded to discover they were drinking black coffee and a plain soda. I was actually offended when I found out they did not drink at all.

"What's wrong with you?" I asked.

One responded, "I am so glad you asked. Have you ever heard of Alcoholics Anonymous?"

I hadn't, so these two men, Chad and Lucky, shared their stories with me and told me that if I went to AA, I would find a way to live sober without ever having to feel hopeless, lost, and defeated again.

The next morning I attended my first AA meeting in Calexico. Fear took a back seat for that ninety minutes. I was safe, and I was home. For the first time in more years than I could recall, I felt a stirring of hope.

For the next month or so, I stayed on couches in the homes of accommodating AAs. Then some women in AA convinced me to enter a recovery house for alcoholic women, so I placed my daughter in foster care for eighteen months and went. I attended AA meetings almost daily, got a job, and went to school. I spent weekends with my daughter and closely followed the suggestions of my sponsor.

The recovery home had assigned me a sponsor. Esther F. was a stern, outspoken World War II nurse who had joined AA in 1944 but went in and out for five years before sobering up for good in 1949. She used to visit with co-founder Bill W. and his wife, Lois, when they came to San Diego to see Bill's mother, Emily Strobel, in the 1950s. Esther tended to be impatient, but in time our relationship became very much like a mother and child's, until she died of cancer, sober, in 1968.

Another strong woman I met was Rosa B., who joined AA in 1945. In 1946, she married Jim B., who had joined AA in 1938 and was responsible for the phrase "God as we understand Him" in our Third Step. Jim's story, "The Vicious Cycle," is in the second and third editions of the Big Book, and reprinted in the book *Experience, Strength & Hope*. Jim was the Panel 4 delegate from our area to the General Service Conference. Rosa later became our Panel 16 delegate.

I once visited Rosa because a man in AA with considerable sobriety, who presented himself as a friend, had made sexual advances toward me. I was distraught.

After listening to my tirade, Rosa made a speech that went something like this: "Listen. Some men, when they were drinking, were no-good, dishonest, untrustworthy, drunken creeps. When they get sober, they become no-good, dishonest, untrustworthy, sober creeps. You have to work your program and keep your eyes peeled for those guys because they will always be out there. AA does not change the world. It changes you and how you respond to the world, and it only does that if you follow the directions of your trusted sponsor, who gets her information from the program as it is written. Now, it's over. Don't make the same mistake twice. Watch to see if others are walking the way they are talking. If they aren't, then smile, be polite, and move on."

That is the way it was then. We got clear, simple, honest directions for one-day-at-a-time living. AA was small, with fewer than 100 meetings in my county. And there was no time for "baby-sitting." All the winners were pretty direct and to the point, because they had lives to live and jobs to go to, and had no time for drama or nonsense. It was sobriety on a shoestring, and recovery was regarded for what it is: a life-and-death situation. There was no time for convincing anyone against their will. The AA of that day was for those who desperately wanted and needed recovery.

Most of the men were very kind, though. I remember in particular Joe C., a successful cabinet maker who came West on an orphan train in the early part of the twentieth century. He had attempted to sober up with the Keeley Cure, and finally joined AA in the 1940s. Joe asked me if I wanted to stay sober one day at a time for the rest of my life. I said yes, and he helped me learn to read again because my brain had become so scrambled by alcohol and pills.

Most AA members were considerably older than me, and they did not know what to make of me. They were not sure it was possible for a teenaged girl to be serious about recovery. Over time, however, my erratic alcoholic personality convinced them I was truly one of the gang!

At that time there was a group called the 20-40 Group. The only members who could speak were those between twenty and forty years old. If you were over forty, you could attend but you couldn't speak, and they couldn't imagine anyone under twenty joining AA. So, I was not allowed inside; I had to sit outside on the porch and listen. Later, this group evolved into a young peoples' group and welcomed AAs of all ages.

One of the aspects of AA I think we've lost over the years is some level of self-respect. Because we were a subculture of sorts, we were careful to be prompt for meetings, to dress as if we were attending work or church, to be attentive during meetings, to not hold side conversations during someone else's sharing, and to hold each other in high regard. Sometimes, when I go to meetings today I see general confusion; people are getting up and milling around and talking to one another during another person's share, and I feel sad and like a dinosaur. Now that AA is a household word and the Twelve Steps have been adapted to address almost every form of social problem, the trade-off may be the casual attitude, expressed in dress and language.

One of the most positive changes I've noticed in the past forty-one years is a higher level of public awareness. As with all things in life, there is growth and growth brings change. One thing remains constant: Sobriety is a gift, a treasure to be cherished, a state of existence that cannot be maintained without the grace of God or a Higher Power guiding each person one day at a time as we "trudge the Road of Happy Destiny."

AA found me. I found a new life in AA, a life filled with challenge, promise, and hope. There have been many times when I've felt inadequate to meet life's demands, but AA and the Twelve Steps have always helped me find a way. I continue to sponsor women in AA and attend meetings regularly, including a Step study group. I love Alcoholics Anonymous. I love and cherish my life in recovery. My fervent prayer for each and every one of us is that AA will be there, one day at a time, forever.

FAIRLEIGH M.
LA MESA, CALIFORNIA

EXPERIENCE SOBRIETY
DEAR GRAPEVINE, FEBRUARY 2011

I thought my life was over when I was forced into rehab at the age of 17. I could not fathom not picking up a drink again. But then, I realized that I only need to take my sobriety and my life one day at a time. With that mentality, I've managed to put together 101 days of sobriety—the best 101 days of my life.

The gifts of sobriety have already begun to blow my mind. I was admitted to one of the best colleges in America, and my relationship with my family has flourished. I've also found my God in the rooms, which I never thought would happen. I am changing for the better every day. I'm alive, and that's exhilarating.

Whenever I listen to old-timers speak about the horror that came along with drinking and using drugs, it makes me want to stay sober even more. AA has potentially saved my life. I hope this message encourages another teenager to experience sobriety. Thank you, Grapevine, for the messages you deliver every month.

JUSTIN M.
NEWARK, NEW JERSEY

R-E-S-P-E-C-T
JULY 2000

I recently had the pleasure of attending a young peoples' conference hosted by members of my home group. It was the typical young peoples' conference experience: Energy and emotions ranged between extremes, from excitement and hilarity to a profound and reverent understanding of the seriousness of this disease. And I got lots and lots of hugs. Hugging has become the staple of conferences, and, indeed, of AA in general. Though some groups and some areas avoid this custom, I usually can count on a few embraces at any meeting. This is, as far as I know, an AA phenomenon. Newcomers and visitors are usually a little shocked and uncomfortable at first, but touch can have the power to make a lonely alcoholic feel very welcome and loved, maybe for the first time in a long time.

Sometime in the past (before my time in AA), organizers of young peoples' conferences introduced a mechanism to spread this good cheer: the "warm fuzzy." It consists of a mass of short yarn pieces bound up into a ball and hung around the neck with a long string. Here's how it works: you approach a fellow AA member, hug him or her, pull a string out of your ball, and tie it onto their long string. A much-loved part of conferences, the custom of exchanging warm fuzzies has spawned related practices, including that of offering a marble in exchange for a hug.

Sounds like fun, doesn't it? It is. Most of the time. But I have seen some exceptions. Here is an example: At last weekend's conference, I was serving as a greeter at the door for a meeting when a fellow approached and offered me a marble. When I cheerfully and politely declined to accept it, he told me that I was very rude and should buzz off. Imagine my surprise! A moment ago didn't he want to hug me? This confirmed something that I had suspected for a long time: Saying "yes" to a hug doesn't always mean surrendering to a loving, accepting, or even safe, embrace. The more I thought about it, the more disturbed I became. For one thing, why did he approach me, a twenty-three-year-old girl in a short dress and lipstick, and not the older man standing beside me, also a door greeter? I fully understand that this young man does not speak for AA or young peoples' conferences, nor perhaps for the sober person he himself may become in five or ten years. But his reaction does point out a trend that I find troubling: In the eyes of some, it is not okay to say no to a hug. I've had sponsees who confirm this. When these young girls, between the ages of sixteen and twenty and in early sobriety, have to check with their sponsors about whether or not it is all right to refuse a hug, there is a problem. While hugging is nice, it should be a choice, and no one should ever be made to feel like she owes anyone a hug.

I know I am not alone in this sentiment. Recently, several committees have decided not to use warm fuzzies or other hugging devices at their conferences, for these and other reasons. I cannot speak for these committees or for AA in general, nor do I want to initiate an anti-warm fuzzy or anti-hugging campaign! I also don't assume that I know the answer to this problem. But I think it is a problem, even if there are only a small number of people who attempt to exert unfair pressure on fellow AAs. When I came to AA, I was desperate for any kind of attention, and I was fortunate to land in a home group where most of the men refused to take advantage of my loneliness and vulnerability. These men did for me what I could not do for myself. They kept me safe from predatory behavior in all its subtle forms, at least in the rooms of AA. This is why it is important for me to share this concern now. I hope to always have hugs in my life, but I also want to feel comfortable in refusing them, especially in AA. We learn in elementary school that we have the right to say "no" to any kind of touch. I don't want AA to be a place where that right is lost. Put another way, I am responsible for the hand of AA to always be there, but that does not include the rest of my body.

BRENNA M.
SALT LAKE CITY, UTAH

AN ARCHWAY TO LIFE
JANUARY 2009

I was introduced to AA at age sixteen, and somehow managed to stay sober through my senior year in high school and actually graduate on time. It was a rule in my household that we attend at least two years of a community college before transferring to a four-year institution. At the time, it seemed like some kind of punishment. All I wanted to do was get away and live on my own. Looking back I was lucky my parents had such a rule. I was able to stay in the area where I got sober, and establish a firm foundation before moving and becoming immersed in a college setting.

I remember the fears and concerns that I had about applying for and going away to college. I was terrified about living on campus and trying to stay sober in a party environment. I had done a lot of my partying and drinking with my older sister and her college friends, so I thought I knew what to expect. My experience was that alcohol was everywhere, and that it was the center of a college student's existence.

I went through the process of applying for colleges, and, after an interview at a small college in Greensboro, North Carolina, I decided that this was the place to finish my college education. I remember traveling the six hours to Greensboro. My head was swimming with concerns.

How would the interview go? Would they like me? If I liked the school and got accepted, how would I manage being separated from my AA friends, my home group, my sponsor, and my network of meetings? I had listened enough in meetings to know that wherever we go we take our Higher Power with us, but my faith had not caught up with my thinking.

When I arrived at the college, the miracle began to happen. I set foot on campus, and, for the first time in my recovery, I was filled with an overwhelming feeling of "this is where I belong." I believe that it was my Higher Power's way of comforting me and guiding me through my fears.

I have since come to realize that moments such as these are rare in sobriety. For me it was the begining of a true turning point in my sobriety and way of thinking. I began to be willing and trust in God and embrace the Third Step. I was accepted to the college, and, despite my fears, the miracles kept happening. I was sure that the only way I would survive the rest of college was to live off campus. In my mind there was no way I could live on campus in a dorm and not drink.

Well, as usual, my Higher Power had other plans. I was not permitted to live off campus. At the time I was angry and distraught. My self-centeredness took over. "Why are they doing this to me? Don't they understand? What if my roommate wants to drink and party all the time?"

As time passed, I was able to gain some measure of acceptance about my circumstances. I knew what I had to do. Upon my arrival in Greensboro, I started going to meetings right away. I got a meeting list and began to establish a meeting schedule that worked with my class schedule.

I soon fell in love with Greensboro AA. My concerns about my roommate were also resolved rather quickly. It turned out that the dorm I was placed in was not a typical dorm. It was quiet, and most of the partying was done at other areas on campus. One evening, about two weeks into the semester, my roommate confronted me. She said, "Do you not like me?" I didn't understand why she was asking such a question. "Of course I like you. What made you think I didn't?"

She was worried because I went out every evening, and she thought it was because I didn't want to spend time with her. I realized that it was time to share with her about my involvement with AA. She was very much relieved, and that night she shared with me something about her lifestyle that she had been afraid to share. We are very close friends to this day.

I loved my college experience. I would not change anything about it. In addition to a wonderful education, I received many wonderful lessons in life. I gained lifelong friends both in and out of AA. I learned that one of the gifts of recovery is that members of AA are given the opportunity to live and face life. Today I have the tools to meet any situation.

God willing, I will soon celebrate my eighteenth anniversary, and I have walked through many experiences sober. I have lived abroad, received an advanced degree, gotten married, and had a baby. For me, going away to college was the completion of the archway. I was able to walk through and gain the tools to continue to live a happy, productive, and sober life.

KATE C.
HADDON HEIGHTS, NEW JERSEY

CHAPTER NINE

A FEW 24 HOURS LATER

*Young old-timers talk about where their journey has taken
them, and about passing it on to the next generation*

"When I joined AA, I had a fantasy—to be the white-haired old coot at the back of the room, banging my cane on the table and telling all you young whipper-snappers what it was like back in the good old days, when we did it right, you understand," writes the author of "Surviving the Fall."

AA anniversaries are important milestones. When we move into the teen years of our recovery, then the twenties, as sober alcoholics, we may be quietly amazed. We sometimes think we can still taste that particular old favorite on our tongue, but we have not picked it up despite anything life has thrown us. As they say in the rooms, "I didn't drink, and I got old." The anniversary celebration thrown by a home group shows the next generation that they, too, can stay sober—one day at a time—for a few 24 hours.

One author says that as she approaches her twenty-third year sober, "my Higher Power has brought me farther than I could ever have imagined. And AA has allowed me to walk through all life has had to offer—good, bad, or indifferent. I am grateful I was able to get sober as a teenager and grow up in AA."

These AAs talk about the struggles that continue in life, that no one is immune to, sober or not. But nearly everyone writes that they are blessed to have the support of AA friends, a Higher Power of their own understanding, and a plan for living. "Sometimes I am jealous that others got to drown the feelings of such experiences in a bottle," an author writes. "Some days, I wonder if I wasn't just a teenager who was experimenting with alcohol, not a real alcoholic. And daily, I thank my Higher Power for giving me the strength not to pick up that first drink and find out."

WHO SAYS AN OLD-TIMER'S GOT TO BE OLD?
APRIL 2001

I'm not sure what defines an old-timer. Some say ten years of sobriety, others say twenty years. Still others say only the original members were old-timers. I hit the ten-year mark when I was twenty-six years old. Now I'm thirty and have fourteen years of recovery. I don't feel like an old-timer, but I do have a different perspective on some things in recovery.

I never fell off a barstool or danced on the bar. I never got a drunk-driving ticket or totaled a car. I got my driver's license, finished high school, graduated from college, and became "of age" in sobriety. I never cheated on a spouse in a drunken blackout, nor spent my last couple of dollars on a drink instead of diapers. I went through a marriage, the birth of two children, divorce, bankruptcy, a second marriage, the birth of my third child, and the death of that child all in sobriety. Sometimes I am jealous that others got to drown the feelings of such experiences in a bottle. Some days, I wonder if I wasn't just a teenager who was experimenting with alcohol, not a real alcoholic. And daily, I thank my Higher Power for giving me the strength not to pick up that first drink and find out.

Today, through doing the Fourth Step, I know that I was by no means a high-bottom drunk. I drank from the time I was old enough to toddle up to the table and finish off what some "normal" drinker had left in the glass. I was thirteen years old the first time I went out in search of a drink. I drank until I was drunk, threw up, blacked out, passed out, and woke up in a strange place. Before even asking where I was, I asked where the booze was. But I continued to try to drink enough to get to that place again, on an almost daily basis for the next three years. I thought that for the first time in my life I fit in: I was funny, people liked me, and I was having fun. That "fun" took me to

places I only had read about or seen on the news. I was a teenage alcoholic runaway, and my life consisted of waking up, finding a drink,
and avoiding being beaten, raped, or shot long enough to pass out and
come to the next morning and start over again. I remember thinking
that I would probably not live to see my eighteenth birthday. But I was
having too much "fun" to quit drinking.

I had my first experience with AA at age fifteen, when family members saw how close to death I was and institutionalized me. I was allowed to attend in-house AA meetings. I had no problem admitting I
was an alcoholic, but I didn't want to quit. I ran away from the hospital
in my hospital pajamas, and walked the streets until someone picked
me up and got me drunk. I had them drop me off at the hospital because I didn't know where I was or where I could sleep that night. I
couldn't stay sober, even in an institution.

After leaving the hospital, I spent the next few weeks in my bedroom
at home, sneaking out only for booze or a bottle of medicine with a high
alcohol content. Then one day I walked out on the porch, looked up to
the sky, and yelled at God. I told him that I knew I was dying and that I
didn't want to die. I told him that I couldn't stay sober by myself and that
he had better put me somewhere I could. I cried for the first time since I
was a young child. When I walked back into the house, my grandmother, with whom I was living, told me she had just talked with someone
at a recovery house for teens; we had an appointment the next day. She
also told me that there were no beds available; this was just an interview.

The next day I slid into the recovery house past a girl carrying a
suitcase. After taking a look at me, the director took only minutes to
offer me her bed. That was October 15, 1985, and I have not had to
have a drink since.

I stayed in the recovery house for over a year, went to one or two
meetings a day, got a sponsor, and learned how to work the Steps. And
before I knew it, for the first time in my life I really was having fun.

Being a teenager with a couple of years of sobriety can be like being
a poster child for young alcoholics. I never had a problem finding a
job at a recovery house or hospital for teenagers, and occasionally my

sponsor just couldn't help herself and would introduce me as "Lisa, who got sober when she was sixteen." I have been on more than one Twelfth Step call to women twenty years my senior who stared at me with a look that said, "This young girl can't possibly know anything about my life." I have been to many meetings where greeters have welcomed me and asked how long I had been sober, only to drop their jaws when I told them.

Don't get me wrong: I am not whining. Frequently I have basked in the attention I received for being such an anomaly. However, my ego was held in check by what seemed an eternity of cleaning ashtrays, making coffee, and wondering why no one ever asked me to sponsor her. One woman who had asked everyone in town to sponsor her at one time or another was finally honest enough to tell me that she felt weird about having a sponsor ten years younger than her. Yet I continued to do whatever I could to be of service, work the program, and discover who I was and what my place was in AA. I knew I had a place here. For the first time, I truly felt that I belonged.

LISA B.
PETALUMA, CALIFORNIA

SOBER IN SCHOOL
DEAR GRAPEVINE, SEPTEMBER 2007

I wanted to say thank you for the articles about youth in sobriety ("AAs on Campus," September 2007). I got sober when I was sixteen and in high school. The articles brought back memories of those early days.

This year I celebrated twenty years of sobriety and I am so grateful that I didn't have to spend any more of my life in misery than I already had. I am continually amazed at how the program works if I work it.

STEPHANIE S.
VALLEY CENTER, KANSAS

RAILROADED
JULY 2010

My sobriety date is April 7, 1986. I was 17 years old in 1986. I'd had my first drink at age 8 and started to use drugs at 9. I now have a life I believe would have never happened if it weren't for Alcoholics Anonymous.

When I first came in, it was difficult for someone my age to feel accepted and to want to be a part of something so big. I went to a treatment center first, but was introduced to AA the first night there. There were no adolescent centers at the time.

I didn't have a desire to stop drinking and never thought that I would stay sober for any period of time. My counselor, for whom I will be eternally grateful, was sober in AA for seven years. She spent two hours a day with me, which was three times more than any counselor spent with any of the other clients. Trust me, I didn't want to be there! She made me read three stories in the Big Book: "Too Young," "A Teen-Ager's Decision" and "Freedom From Bondage." She explained the malady of the disease and she explained to me that I was there because I had a disease. She also said that if I could get sober and stay sober I would be able to help many more young people who were going to come to AA.

When I left to go home, I had no intention to stay sober or help anyone. I went back to a small town in the Midwest, where I was introduced to a new AA group. I wasn't welcomed very well because I am dually addicted. I would share about both addictions and they would share that they were "real alcoholics." I didn't read that part in the Big Book about a real alcoholic. I was asked to leave that group—I was physically removed—and was told not to come back until I could talk about my alcoholism.

Knowing what I have learned today about the Traditions, I wish someone had taken me aside and explained Tradition One and Tradition Two. I didn't come back to another AA meeting until almost eight months later, when I moved to the Central Valley in California. I met my sponsor a few weeks later. God put a young punk kid and a grown man who didn't have a son together. For the next 20 years that man showed me the Twelve Steps and Twelve Traditions. He had me get a service sponsor for the Twelve Concepts for world service. But I didn't like AA for over a year and wouldn't admit that I was an alcoholic for that period of time.

What happened was that I was railroaded into being an alternate general service rep when I was sober for a year and a half. I was 19. At an assembly, a lady who was a district committee member gave a report, during which she said that she sobered up at 20 years old and had 10 years of sobriety. Again, God put the exact person in my life. I didn't understand anything they were talking about. All I knew was that there was a lady who'd gotten sober young, and I was amazed. When I left that weekend I had the desire to stay sober and I was ready to admit that I was an alcoholic. In fact, I wanted what she had and I got the bug for general service. I came back home with a fire that hasn't left me. I was on a mission.

The day my counselor said to me that I could help so many young people if I stayed sober rings true every day of my life. I got involved in my home group, and started speaking at schools and at youth corrections facilities and juvenile institutions.

I still have the energy and the love for AA that was given to me by my sponsor, who passed away almost three years ago with over 30 years of sobriety. At the age of 41, I'm now almost 24 years sober and still involved in general service.

SHAUN G.
MANTECA, CALIFORNIA

MAKING THE GRADE
JULY 1996

I was a full-blown alcoholic by the time I reached college. I did my heaviest, most dangerous drinking at this time. Blackouts were a routine occurrence, so much so that my friends and I joked about having to piece together what we'd done the previous night. Promiscuous, bizarre, and violent behavior was the norm for me when drunk, which was almost daily. I began having the horrifying experience of waking up in a strange place, not knowing whose house I was in, what town I was in, or how I got there. Even though I was usually able to laugh and joke about my escapades, I really wished I could walk around campus with a paper bag over my head because I was so ashamed of my behavior.

Most of my friends drank like I did. Those who didn't sooner or later joined the ranks of people I'd alienated over the course of my drinking career. One day a friend came up to me and said, "I think I might be an alcoholic." I said, "I think I might be one too." She asked me if I'd like to go with her to an AA meeting and I agreed. It was 1983 and I was twenty years old.

Of course I had to have a few beers before I went. We attended a speaker meeting. The speaker was about sixty years old, male, and when I took my first look at him, I wondered what I could possibly have in common with him. I was prepared to ridicule and crack jokes about what he said but I couldn't. Although his circumstances were different, his message hit me in the gut. I knew right then and there that I was an alcoholic. My friend and I, however, left the meeting and went out drinking as usual.

But I had a nagging feeling that I should go back. I didn't realize it, but the meeting we'd attended was in a halfway house. I returned to the meeting solo, having again imbibed prior to my arrival. I must have shown some outward sign of intoxication because the counselor spotted me immediately and requested that I come to his office with him. Calmly, gently, and without judgment, he spoke to me about alcoholism and AA. I can't recall exactly what he said, but I do remember going over the twenty questions with him. I could answer affirmatively to about fifteen of the twenty. A yes answer to more than three says that you are definitely an alcoholic. I knew it was true. The counselor gave me an AA schedule book and I took it because I knew I'd be needing it someday. I have it to this day.

Meanwhile, peer pressure and the disease convinced me that I still had some good years of partying left and that AA could wait until things got worse. Also, I thought my family would be humiliated if it was known I was in AA. It didn't occur to me that my family would be more humiliated if they knew about my drunken behavior and that the money they were paying for my education was being wasted. How I managed to graduate with halfway decent grades is still a mystery to me.

I wanted to wait, to postpone AA until things got worse. They did. I didn't go to another AA meeting for six years. By that time, I was drinking heavily on a daily basis, and was very sick physically, mentally, and spiritually. I looked at those twenty questions again. I could now respond affirmatively to all twenty. I won the prize—a sober, useful life!

I'm grateful for that early experience of AA during college. It says in the "Twelve and Twelve" that "when one alcoholic had planted in the mind of another the true nature of his malady, that person could never be the same again." It could have taken decades for me to get to AA, had I not known that "there is a solution" from my first introduction to the Fellowship back in 1983.

SHEILA N.
NEW BRITAIN, CONNECTICUT

SURVIVING THE FALL
MAY 1998

made my first AA meeting in south Texas in March or April 1971, at the age of thirteen. My parents were in the middle of a nasty divorce, complete with shotguns and butcher knives, and Dad was trying to get sober. His motives at the time weren't very good. He was trying to win the custody fight, and his lawyer and social worker both said that if he quit drinking for a while and went to AA, it might look better to the judge. They thought it would look even better if he took his kids to Alateen and open AA meetings, so that's how I ended up at the meeting. I'd been drinking and taking drugs for about a year, and had experienced blackouts and hangovers. My first drunk, at twelve, was most of a half-gallon of chianti.

When I went to that first AA meeting, I realized almost immediately that I had a problem with alcohol. The speaker was three or four times my age, and had drunk for longer than I'd been alive, but he hit me between the eyes with parts in his story. I stole my first beginner's chip out of the box in the lectern after the meeting a few weeks later.

The idea that I had a problem with alcohol didn't bother me. Both of my parents drank heavily, and it seemed the normal thing to do. Drinking gave me instant relief during the crisis that had led up to the divorce. I'm not sure that I would have lived through the insanity, both mine and my parents', had I not started drinking.

Alcohol didn't do things to me at first, it did things for me. The stress in the house before the divorce was so bad that I was walking around babbling to myself and starting conversations with strangers. People thought I was nuts, and so did I. The drinking and drugs gave me an immediate group of friends, at least a group of people who tolerated my insanity and let me hang around with them. This let me escape from my family, and the wine and marijuana let me not feel for a while. At least I wasn't alone, even if I was crazy.

However, what I ran into at those first AA meetings fascinated me. Here was a group of people who knew what it was like to have Dad come in at three A.M., put pork chops in the broiler, pass out, and then have to put out the fire and air out the house. Obviously, they hadn't read about it in a book, either. Even more important, they weren't there any more. They even seemed to want me around. It had been a long time since I'd been anything but tolerated by my friends.

I realized that to be accepted here I'd have to stop drinking, at least most of the time, but I didn't understand the progressive, fatal nature of alcoholism. I also suffered from the illusion that "organic alkaloids" weren't a problem for alcoholics. After some more trouble (I was arrested for possession of marijuana that summer), I actually did quit drinking and taking drugs by the time I was fourteen and a half. The divorce became final, and Dad, now sober, won custody of the kids. AA and Alateen gave me a place to share, and slowly, over a few years, I began to function in reality.

We moved to California in 1973, and I went to a progressive, highly competitive high school. Amazingly, I ran into a group of friends there who didn't drink or take drugs, and whose parents were Ph.D. mathematicians, physicists, and computer scientists at a government laboratory in town. They accepted me into their group, and I discovered that I still had a few brain cells left. My grades went up to straight As; I learned to play chess, bridge, and poker; and I eventually graduated from high school with honors. I still needed to tie one on occasionally, but the craving for more would be gone when I woke up the next day. I learned quickly that if there wasn't enough for me at a party, it wasn't worth starting.

Meanwhile, there was something in the back of my head called "as soon as ..." As soon as I graduate from high school. As soon as I turn eighteen and the arrest record goes away. As soon as I can afford a car. "As soon as" arrived right before my eighteenth birthday when I got an invitation from my oldest brother to "get in a little trouble with him in Oklahoma." This turned into a four-month-long drinking binge. I ended up breaking all the promises I'd ever made to myself about drinking: I would never drive under the influence of alcohol; I would never show up at work under the influence; I would never borrow things from people without their permission and not return them (I call that "stealing" today); I would never take opiates; I would never spend the paycheck before paying the rent.

Beyond all the broken promises to myself, there was one thing that never went away. From the time I started on that binge I knew that I was an alcoholic. Starting about the end of the first month I tried desperately to stop and I couldn't do it. The craving for more never went away. Gritting my teeth and hanging on, I could make a day or two, no longer. I started taking drinks when I meant well and was trying hard, again and again. My last drink, in January 1976, came after I'd promised myself I'd stay sober that night. Twenty minutes later I had a drink in my hand, half an inch out of it, and no excuse for my behavior. I bought the idea that I couldn't control my drinking that night, without reservation, and I haven't had a drink since.

I started back to AA at two or three days sober, in a run-down, low-bottom AA club. I'd been a straight A student eight months before and now I couldn't complete a sentence without forgetting what I intended to say. This didn't shut me up in meetings, and I was told to sit down and shut up a lot. Occasionally, I hear someone in the same shape I was in (I call it "spinning") and it still can shake me up to remember how messed up I was.

At this point I ran into a group of men who'd been watching me for quite some time. They scared me when they talked in meetings, since they seemed able to look right through me. However, their lives worked and I was approaching emotional collapse, so I started following them around. They pointed me at the Big Book, and insisted that without taking the Steps I would never maintain sobriety, much less get a happy sobriety. I was desperate and I made my first pass through the Steps in six weeks. I did it again about two months later, and have done it again formally four or five times since then. I'm living proof that the Steps do work. After that first pass through them, for the first time in my life I began to feel like I was a normal human being. I was no longer afraid that I'd get struck drunk. I went back to school (dorms are amazing places to live sober!) and finished a degree. I've been self-supporting by my own contributions for years now. Over twenty-one years have passed, I'm still sober, and I'm approaching my fortieth birthday.

I'm back in school working on a Master's degree, and this summer, the university I attend asked me if I would teach a course for them. I was terrified, but I know from AA that if I stay sober and honest, I'll have opportunities placed in front of me. Today it's possible to go anywhere and become anything, as long as I'm willing to do the work. I can even think in terms of getting my Ph.D. someday, maybe even becoming a professor. Maybe. But just for today, I get to grade midterm exams, and take them, too.

When I joined AA, I had a fantasy with which I'll close. My fantasy was to be the white-haired old coot at the back of the room, banging my cane on the table and telling all you young whipper-snappers what it was like back in the good old days, when we did it right, you understand. If I live an average life span of seventy-three years and stay sober, I'll have fifty-five years of sobriety when I die. Today, I believe my old fantasy has a chance to come true.

KEITH M.
LIVERMORE, CALIFORNIA

GRATITUDE LANE
DEAR GRAPEVINE, APRIL 2004

The January 2004 article about ICYPAA (International Conference of Young People in AA) brought to mind many memories of the ICYPAA conferences I have had the privilege to attend.

I started out on my AA path three weeks prior to my twenty-first birthday. In my first AA meeting, I found hope that I could live a life free of the chaos, fear, and dysfunction. But it was at my first ICYPAA in Chicago in 1984 that I came to believe that my future could be filled with unlimited possibilities. This belief came from large-scale and very visible evidence—seeing thousands of sober young people together in one place, many with stories of extraordinary sober lives.

That weekend turned out to be the turning point in my early sobriety. Not only was I "pumped up" (a sensation known as a "conference high"), but I wanted to learn more about the Steps, service, and the Twelve Traditions and Twelve Concepts. So within two weeks of returning home, several of us started a bid committee for our state young peoples' conference. I ended up spending the next ten years extremely involved in conferences in three different states, not to mention serving as a GSR, DCM, and area committee member. I wanted to give back what had been given to me at my first ICYPAA.

Now, almost twenty years later, I still go to young peoples' conferences when I can, although I have been blessed with several exciting careers, a beautiful wife, and three incredible children who keep my life full and rich.

DAVE S.
INDIANAPOLIS, INDIANA

YOUNG, DRUNK AND BROKE
JANUARY 2011

I grew up in a family environment that was riddled with both alcoholism and drug addiction. As far back in my memory as I can go, I remember my mom or some other parental figure drinking or using some type of drugs. By the age of 12, drinking alcohol was something everyone did everywhere, all the time.

This was also when my mom decided she needed help and went to AA. She often took me along with her while she attended meetings and I hung out playing pool in the room below the meeting. By age 15 I was attending Alateen on a regular basis and by 17 was going on and off to AA for myself. I ended up in a treatment facility after overdosing on drugs and drinking a massive amount of hard liquor.

My stay in that facility was my first real attempt to stay sober, though I was not completely convinced I had a serious problem and I found sobriety fleeting at best. I relapsed one more time and this time I found myself in even more serious trouble. I was arrested with a case of cheap beer and a lot of illegal drugs. It turned out that the arresting officer knew my family (who by now lived in another state) and convinced my parents to take me in one last time, on the condition that I stay sober when I arrived. I agreed and drove to the city where my parents were living, ready to start my new life in AA.

I attended an AA meeting there that day only to find the members were all at least 30 years my senior. I was 18 years old, in a retirement community, trying to get sober. I used the "I am too young" excuse and in a short time found myself on the streets again.

This time everything was different. I found I no longer had any control whatsoever—I couldn't stop for any reason. This relapse lasted for about seven months and in that time I hit the bottom of the barrel. I ended up staying in a dumpster behind a fast-food restaurant because I couldn't afford a hotel room. Even at this level I didn't believe AA would work for me; after all, I had been in and out of AA for the last few years. AA didn't work for people like me—people my age.

Then one day I had a very different thought shoot through my mind—if I didn't stop drinking I was going to die. It didn't matter if AA worked or not; I needed help. So I decided to give AA meetings one last shot. I got a hotel room and stayed sober for the next few days. One evening, all the street friends I had showed up at my door and brought drinks and drugs. That night I couldn't get drunk or loaded no matter how much I put into my body. I told my friends it would be the last time I ever drank with them and asked them all to leave and not come back.

That was Jan. 7, 1982, the day that turned out to be my sobriety date. I had just turned 19. When I walked into the AA meeting place again, the same old people were there and they all welcomed me back. I sat just long enough to hear the beginning of Chapter 5 of the Big Book. It was like someone had hit me on the head with a club—every word applied to me. That was almost 29 years ago now and Chapter 5 still has the same impact today.

Being sober in 1982 at 19 was such a very lonely experience; it's almost hard to describe. Everyone I met my age was in the midst of the "wild life." In my entire city there were only three other AA members under 21 and none of us liked each other. When I faced problems in AA and asked other members for help, they would just look at me and tell me, "When I was your age I was drunk! Sorry, I don't know what to tell you—you're going to have to figure it out yourself." Well I did, often with horrible results. I often share that I have made all the same mistakes any other person has made, either in AA or not. Only I couldn't say, "Yeah, I did that, but I was drunk when I did it." I had to admit that I made those same mistakes sober and had to stand up and be accountable for my actions later. I found it was all just a part of growing up, only I grew up in AA, literally.

I stayed through the end of my teens, through my 20s, through my 30s, and now through most of my 40s. I didn't just read the Twelve Steps, Twelve Traditions and Twelve Concepts; I have made them a part of my life and learned to live their principles. My life today is absolutely incredible.

Because I got sober so young, I am able to reach just about any young person who walks into AA and let them know that AA will work at their age, that alcohol doesn't see age, sex or heritage—it's an equal opportunity destroyer. I usually direct them to the local Young People in AA meetings and also try getting them involved in our Local Young Peoples' Committee, which supports other larger state young peoples' conferences. In California it's ACYPAA, which stands for All California Young People in Alcoholics Anonymous, something that I had the privilege to chair here in 1999. Two years ago our area was awarded the ACYPAA conference again, and with an entirely new group of young people running it, became the largest ACYPAA conference to date. I have literally watched a fellowship rise around me. Today there are several thousand "young people" members in this state alone, something I never dreamed I would see. Today I am a part of a growing number of once young people in AA who have stayed sober for many years and found a life, and lifestyle, that is so far beyond anything I could have ever hoped to have all those years ago when I stumbled back into AA for the last time.

JAMIE L.
OCEANSIDE, CALIFORNIA

GOOD, BAD, OR INDIFFERENT
JULY 2008

was first introduced to AA in March 1984, at the age of fifteen, after I got out of a rehab facility. The next nine months I tried to play the good AA member so I could go home. I went to meetings, I went to Big Book studies, I parroted what old-timers said, and I felt like I was succeeding at pulling the wool over everyone's eyes, that I was getting away with it.

Around Christmas 1984, I was visiting my parents for the week. After we had lunch Christmas day, I asked my mom when I could come home. She simply said, "You're not. We do not like the person you have become. People are trying to help you and you cannot appreciate it or respect anyone." I stayed quiet. She was right; I was caught, and I was upset. I asked my mother if I could go to a friend's home.

I went over to my friend's home and told him what was wrong. He offered a drink and I took it. Hell, I thought, this sobriety thing is not helping; what's the harm? We drank through most of the night. I vaguely remember leaving his home and going to find another friend, searching for more booze. I had to have more.

I remember bouncing from house to house that night, looking for another drink. My curfew time came and went. I didn't care. Eventually, I made my way home. I snuck in, tripping over bicycles and slamming against the station wagon. I reached for the garage door, to be greeted by an assistant house parent at my group home. I had snuck into the wrong house.

Her name was Ann and she was a member of Al-Anon. She shook her head and told me to take a shower, which I did. I knew I was in serious trouble. I got out of the shower and she called me upstairs and fed me. I remember getting violently ill. She held my head up over the toilet and then fed me some more. After several repeated episodes of this, Ann gave me a glass of orange juice and honey and sent me to bed. Never had she criticized me; she was actually very loving and tolerant.

The next morning, I woke up with a headache. Ann gave me a list of chores to do after breakfast. The whole time, I shook. After I finished, Ann looked at me and plainly said, "You have two choices—go to AA or I tell your judge." I went to a meeting.

I was terrified, for the reality of my problem hit me for the first time in my life. I could not stop drinking when I started. For the first time I came to understand that if I was to live, I could not drink.

That was December 26, 1984. I was sixteen and I have not had a drink since.

I am happy to say that as I approach my twenty-third year of sobriety, my Higher Power has brought me farther than I could ever have imagined. I have four beautiful children and a loving husband. In sobriety, I have learned to deal with jobs, deaths, highs, and lows. And AA has allowed me to walk through all life has had to offer—good, bad, or indifferent. I am grateful I was able to get sober as a teenager and grow up in AA. I have been sober over half my life.

The biggest question I get asked today is: "How does this deal work?" And the answer is simple: "Rarely have we seen a person fail who has thoroughly followed our path." So, to the newcomer: Pocket your pride, get a sponsor, and learn how to follow this path. And to the old-timers: Pocket your pride, pick up newcomers, take them to meetings, and continue to share what was freely given to you.

That is how this deal worked in the beginning, and that's how it works today—one alcoholic helping another stay sober.

MARGARET R.
STEPHENVILLE, TEXAS

THE TWELVE STEPS

1. We admitted we were powerless over alcohol—that our lives had become unmanageable.
2. Came to believe that a Power greater than ourselves could restore us to sanity.
3. Made a decision to turn our will and our lives over to the care of God as we understood Him.
4. Made a searching and fearless moral inventory of ourselves.
5. Admitted to God, to ourselves, and to another human being the exact nature of our wrongs.
6. Were entirely ready to have God remove all these defects of character.
7. Humbly asked Him to remove our shortcomings.
8. Made a list of all persons we had harmed, and became willing to make amends to them all.
9. Made direct amends to such people wherever possible, except when to do so would injure them or others.
10. Continued to take personal inventory and when we were wrong promptly admitted it.
11. Sought through prayer and meditation to improve our conscious contact with God as we understood Him, praying only for knowledge of His will for us and the power to carry that out.
12. Having had a spiritual awakening as the result of these steps, we tried to carry this message to alcoholics, and to practice these principles in all our affairs.

THE TWELVE TRADITIONS

1. Our common welfare should come first; personal recovery depends upon A.A. unity.
2. For our group purpose there is but one ultimate authority—a loving God as He may express Himself in our group conscience. Our leaders are but trusted servants; they do not govern.
3. The only requirement for A.A. membership is a desire to stop drinking.
4. Each group should be autonomous except in matters affecting other groups or A.A. as a whole.
5. Each group has but one primary purpose—to carry its message to the alcoholic who still suffers.
6. An A.A. group ought never endorse, finance or lend the A.A. name to any related facility or outside enterprise, lest problems of money, property, and prestige divert us from our primary purpose.
7. Every A.A. group ought to be fully self-supporting, declining outside contributions.
8. Alcoholics Anonymous should remain forever nonprofessional, but our service centers may employ special workers.
9. A.A., as such, ought never be organized; but we may create service boards or committees directly responsible to those they serve.
10. Alcoholics Anonymous has no opinion on outside issues; hence the A.A. name ought never be drawn into public controversy.
11. Our public relations policy is based on attraction rather than promotion; we need always maintain personal anonymity at the level of press, radio and films.
12. Anonymity is the spiritual foundation of all our traditions, ever reminding us to place principles before personalities.

ALCOHOLICS ANONYMOUS

AA's program of recovery is fully set forth in its basic text, *Alcoholics Anonymous* (commonly known as the Big Book), now in its Fourth Edition, as well as in *Twelve Steps and Twelve Traditions*, *Living Sober*, and other books. Information on AA can also be found on AA's website at www.AA.ORG, or by writing to: Alcoholics Anonymous, Box 459, Grand Central Station, New York, NY 10163. For local resources, check your local telephone directory under "Alcoholics Anonymous." Four pamphlets, "This is A.A.," "Is A.A. For You?," "44 Questions," and "A Newcomer Asks" are also available from AA.

AA GRAPEVINE

AA Grapevine is AA's international monthly journal, published continuously since its first issue in June 1944. The AA pamphlet on AA Grapevine describes its scope and purpose this way: "As an integral part of Alcoholics Anonymous since 1944, the Grapevine publishes articles that reflect the full diversity of experience and thought found within the A.A. Fellowship, as does La Viña, the bimonthly Spanish-language magazine, first published in 1996. No one viewpoint or philosophy dominates their pages, and in determining content, the editorial staff relies on the principles of the Twelve Traditions."

In addition to magazines, AA Grapevine, Inc. also produces books, eBooks, audiobooks, and other items. It also offers a Grapevine Online subscription, which includes: four new stories weekly, AudioGrapevine (the audio version of the magazine), Grapevine Story Archive (the entire collection of Grapevine articles), and the current issue of Grapevine and La Viña in HTML format. For more information on AA Grapevine, or to subscribe to any of these, please visit the magazine's website at www.aagrapevine.org or write to:

AA Grapevine, Inc.
475 Riverside Drive
New York, NY 10115